Approaching Felonias Park

Katherine Mercurio Gotthardt

Thank You!
Katherine Gotthardt

Aberdeen Bay

Harbin - Washington, D.C. - San Diego

Aberdeen Bay
Published by Aberdeen Bay, an imprint of Champion Writers.
www.aberdeenbay.com

PUBLISHER'S NOTE

This is a book of fiction. Names, characters, places, and
incidents are either the product of author's imagination or are
used fictitiously. Any resemblance to actual persons, living or
dead, business establishments, government agencies, events,
or locales is entirely coincidental.

International Standard Book Number
ISBN-13: 978-1-60830-068-6
ISBN-10: 1-60830-068-4

Printed in the United States of America.

With all my heart, I dedicate *Approaching Felonias Park* to my loving husband, David Andrew Gotthardt, who has always encouraged my writing and who nudged me to begin this project, mainly because he thought the dream I had starring the bizarre "bunnymoose" was worth putting into a novel.

Acknowledgements

I have been blessed with so many people who helped me with this book that I cannot possibly list them all here. Suffice to say, if you do not see your name in print, you know who you are, and you know how much I appreciate you.

This book was born of NaNoWriMo, National Novel Writing Month, an online project challenging writers of any level to produce 50,000 words in 30 days. In 2006, after signing up late as a participant, I spat out the first draft of what is now known as Approaching Felonias Park. It was terrible, of course, and I didn't bother with the book until somewhere around 2008, leaving it alone again until 2010, when a writer and editor friend of mine, Bette Hileman, told me I needed to do something with the manuscript. So my first thank-yous go to NaNoWriMo and Bette Hileman.

Bette, you and I both know there is no way a publishing house would have considered my submission had you not edited and formatted the initial document. I will never forget your generosity.

I also want to thank Ross Murphy of Aberdeen Bay for holding the workshop at the local library where I first learned about Aberdeen and the publishing process. Ross, your honesty and thoroughness were helpful, and I am grateful you thought enough of my submission to accept the book for publication.

And to Mom—I know you will be showing this book to anyone standing still longer than five seconds. That's okay, but please do not get arrested for harassment, and please do not give out my phone number.

On a different note, please know, Mom, that you are the reason I began to write. As soon as you taught me to read, I was able to put pen to paper. Without you, I would not have succeeded as a writer and probably would have ended up as an inept food services manager.

To my brother Michael, thank you for believing in me and my stories and for playing Scrabble with me when no one else would. You are a true treasure.

To my husband David, thank you for listening as I read each draft of this acknowledgements page.

In addition, I would like to thank the following who have helped launch me full-throttle into the literary world: Jane Riley, Museum Store Manager, Manassas Museum; Tina Cox, Administrative Assistant, Rev. Nancy McDonald Ladd and congregation at Bull Run Unitarian Universalist Church; Jenn Hoskins, President, Two Dots Marketing; Charles Leggett, Friends Uniting Nokesville; Board and members of Buckland Preservation Society; Ron Dunn, Coordinator for Writers Roundtable; Editors and Staff at *News & Messenger*; Michael Kieffer, Executive Director of Bull Run Mountain Conservancy, and staff at Bull Run Mountains Conservancy; Owner at the blog "Slam Dunks"; Staff at *Caper Literary Journal*; Carol Covin, author of *Granny-Guru*; Wally Covington, Brentsville District Supervisor, Prince William County; Sheila School, Co-Founder, League of Women Voters, Prince William Area; Jane Dvonch and David Montgomery, Prince William Symphony Orchestra; Pam Sackett, Assistant to Wally Covington, Brentsville District Supervisor; Bob Chase, Manager, Prospero's Books; Staff at Prospero's Books; Tara Donaldson, Editor, *Gainesville Times*; Gainesville-Haymarket Rotary Club; Editors at Bristow Enews; Editors at *Washington Examiner*; Clinton Foster, Interviews and Projects blog; Marilyn Karp and the Haymarket Earth Day team; Perely Eaton, LLI Manassas; Monique at peorianow.org; Bill Golden at Prince William Life; Angela Stokes and the folks at Journey Through Hallowed Ground; Dominion Woman's Club; Kathy Bentz and the folks who organized "Arts Alive!"; Matt Brower, Owner, Simply Sweet on Main; Selina Farmer-Williams, Illustrator and Artist; Shane Williams, Book Designer; Cindy Brookshire, Founder of Write by the Rails; members, BRUU Writers' Group; Jennifer Robinson, Gainesville-Haymarket Rotary Community Corps; contributors, Writers for a Cause.

And to the rest of my family, friends and supporters, I send gratitude and love. I hope you enjoy this final version of *Approaching Felonias Park*.

Chapter One

"Hello. My name is Jezabel. I process high-interest loans for the desperate."

That's how Jezabel McPhearson would have described herself.

She would say it in an even, ironic voice and nod patiently, as if the listener understood. But she was feeling neither ironic nor patient this morning. She was feeling lecherous.

In an act of perversion, Jezabel's mother had chosen her daughter's name. Jezabel meant "The Lord (Baal) exists." And for whatever reason, Jezabel's Bible-smart mother thought it a good joke to name her daughter after a pagan sentiment.

But Jezabel's mother also liked the image of the Old Testament figure: though "Jezabel" had become loosely associated with prostitution and evil, Mom thought more of Jezabel's royal rank and how the woman represented a powerful figure behind the throne.

While she maintained a perhaps unhealthy sense of guilt, Jezabel never felt completely evil, nor did she feel powerful, even though she was the giver of money, the loan maker. And she knew she had only a few more moments before the next beggar would be at her office door.

This was the third day Charles had called in sick. Ridiculous, she thought. She might have had more sympathy if he had claimed to have, say, strep throat or something serious. Or even something interesting like, "Hi. I ate a steak from a moo-moo with mad cow disease. I'm recovering nicely but need at least an extra day." She could picture Charles saying that. She couldn't imagine herself coming up with anything so amusing or creative.

But no, she ruminated irritably. He left the message on her voice mail saying he had a virus and probably would not be in for the next three days. Jezabel wondered, could he predict how long he would be throwing up or sitting on the toilet? Could he fortell how long a virus would live in his body? Or was this some kind of scientific guess on his part (which she found equally annoying because neither of them were scientists)?

In fact, the more she worked here, the more she realized how absolutely unscientific this process was, how pointless, how mindless. How long had she had this horrible job? Five years? Six? Seven? She had lost count, and actually, she didn't want to count. Labeling the time with a number would make it worse. Besides, no one could count to infinity.

It's not that she really hated what she did. Well, actually, yes. She really was hating what she was doing. She wanted a change, but she felt more stuck than a nail in a petrified tree. How could she change fields now, especially when she had been working in a strange niche for so long and didn't have the education to break her out of the odd prison of pseudo-lending-and-accounting?

Jezabel hung up her jacket on the wall-mounted hook beside her desk. She stashed her tan vinyl purse in the file drawer and logged back onto her computer. She flicked her long, straight, blond hair over her thin shoulder and wondered why she hadn't put it up in her usual ponytail. Maybe, though, she should consider wearing her hair in a bun. Would she feel more respectable then?

Her computer system came up. On her wallpaper, she and Michael held hands and walked in the little park not far from Jezabel's apartment.

Jezabel loved that picture. The sky smiled in clouds. Michael's brown eyes and grin looked mischievously puppy-like. He didn't have his beard then, and she could read his expression. Her fair hair and complexion contrasted with his tan face and natural, dark waves just long enough for her to run her fingers through. Her own brown eyes smiled. He looked happy, and so did she.

It was bright autumn in the photo, and the trees held those glorious colors that said it would be at least a few more weeks before winter set in for real. Jezabel wished herself back to that day.

Michael. Jessop Michael Pastore. He insisted on being called Michael, which Jezabel could completely understand. It was one thing they had in common — dislike of their first names. If Jezabel had a middle name, she would use hers, too.

Maybe she should think about Michael's idea seriouly this time. What was she so afraid of? Was she worried that his bad habits would make for a bad life? Was she afraid he wouldn't pay the bills or clean the apartment? She had seen his place. It was usually a mess, but then, she wasn't some kind of clean freak. Of course, there was Tarika, and Jezabel didn't want to give up her kitty. And Jezabel liked having her things orderly, like she did now. She just wasn't sure.

Jezabel knew what it meant to her clients that she was there, but part of her just didn't care. It wasn't that she was cold. She just couldn't really afford to be fussy anymore. She was burnt. She was tired. She was bored. And she didn't like how angry she was feeling as a result. It was cancerous.

So here she sat, doodling on the bland calendar that owned most of her desk. She wrote her name. She wrote "Charles," then drew a stick figure of a woman slapping the name silly.

Charles Oro. He liked his name, but at the moment, she wasn't fond of it or him. She would have to take his clients as well as hers, and the lines would be out the door again. For the third day.

She groaned in her head. Thirty or more people a day at her door asking for money. For a loan. At least thirty times, she would have to explain the mission of the organization and their responsibility. She mimicked herself saying it now, murmuring:

"Remember, In-a-Pinch is not a bank. You are taking out a high interest loan to be repaid over a six-month period. You will be responsible for the principal of the loan, monthly interest accrued at 27% and the initiation fee of $75.00. If you miss one or more payments, we reserve the right to aggressively collect from you and/or the cosigners designated on your application form. Do you have any questions?"

This was the part she could say in her sleep, and it was the part that she didn't know how to manage on her resume. How could she describe this on any resume?

"Hello. My name is Jezabel. I process high interest loans for the desperate. How do we manage collections? Well, I don't really get involved in that part of the process. I just take their applications and assess eligibility. Do I know about my company's reputation? I am not sure what you mean by that, Sir."

This was the part that always got her. Hey, it wasn't her fault the way collections were handled. She had a job to do, and collections was not part of it. Besides, clients were always so happy to get their loans. She wasn't responsible for their future misery. She was making them happy at the moment, right?

Tonya stepped through the door and gestured to a woman with back-length curly red hair and saucer-sized, purple-rimmed glasses. The woman's makeup looked spackled on. Her purple lipstick was peeling, and the concealer barely covered the giant pockmarks that looked like left-overs from childhood chicken pox. Jezabel sighed again. Thank God she had been one of the lucky generations to receive the inoculation. She had her problems, but giant pockmarks were not included in them.

"This is…" Tonya began. Jezabel nodded and smiled the same way she might at a party where she didn't know anyone.

Jezabel tried never to pay attention to their names. There were too many of them and, unless they forgot to sign something correctly, in which case they had to come back to see her, Jezabel never saw them more than once anyway. Why waste mental energy memorizing names that meant nothing in the long run? And did she want to think about them having names? Wasn't that like naming a fish, a no-no because when the fish died, you would miss it?

Social security numbers and filled out forms were what she looked for. Sure, she couldn't help but remember a name or two if the client went to collections, but it was never a surprise when a loan went to collections. More than half of the clients went that route.

So Jezabel busied herself by looking at the woman's polyester, paisley-print shirt. Orange and teal mega-print and orange pants. Purple boots. The red hair big and sprayed. A lopsided smile. The woman was tall, and when she sat in the chair in front of Jezabel, she looked uncomfortable, like her big feet didn't know where to put themselves. The woman fidgeted and finally handed over her paperwork to Jezabel who scanned it to make sure all the blanks were filled in. The lady bounced her leg and peered through her big lenses at Jezabel who read and pointed to a section on the form.

"So you are not working right now, is that correct?" Jezabel asked. She had learned to ask this question right off, without hesitation and without apology.

"That's right," said the woman.

"So how do you plan on paying this loan?" Jezabel asked, again, directly.

"I get some assistance and I do some work under the table," the woman said, equally as directly.

Jezabel looked over the paper at the woman. "What kind of work do you do?" she asked.

"I fix fans."

"Oh," said Jezabel, and moved closer to her computer.

"Don't you want to know anything else?" the redhead asked, staring seriously at Jezabel. "Like how many I can fix and why I haven't fixed any in the last month and how I afford the parts and what I do?"

Jezabel shrugged. It wasn't her business to ask for details about the lady's business. She just wanted to know how the bill would get paid.

"See, on trash day, I go through the neighborhoods. It's the weirdest thing. You almost always see a fan in the trash. I've been doing this for ten years now and you want to know what is even weirder?" The lady bounced her leg faster, her face suddenly animated, the makeup cracking even more. "Every year, if I go back to houses that threw out a fan, they have another one at that same house. So you know what that means?"

Jezabel found herself looking at the lady and wondering.

"It means the same people buy cheap fans every year. They use them for a season or two, and then they toss 'em. That's right. Just toss them out like junk!" The woman frowned like she couldn't believe the injustice of it all. "It's like fans are disposable. But what these people don't know is…" Jezabel waited. The woman leaned in closer and lowered her voice to a whisper. "Fans can be restored."

"I see," said Jezabel, who turned back to her computer, mentally slapping herself for being taken in by the story, as if something exciting was going to come of it.

"So I collect all the fans, and I take some apart to replace the broken parts of the other ones. Then when people bring me their fans to fix, I have one to sell them or I have the part to replace theirs. Pretty nice, huh?"

"Yes, sounds like a good kind of business you've got going there," Jezabel said flatly, entering the information into the computer.

"Yup. I get ten dollars usually for fixing a fan. It takes me less than an hour and all my parts are free. And I never have to buy tools because I have Daddy's old tools and he had a lot of them." The leg was really bouncing now. The lady was kicking the desk, distracting Jezabel, who wished the woman would just shut up and be still.

"It will be just one more moment, Ma'am, and then I will print up the agreement," Jezabel said. "Do you have any questions on the loan?"

"Nope. I know I will have enough fans to fix in the next month or so because warmer weather is right around the corner. I will get really busy and make lots of money, enough to pay the taxes on the house and this little loan back."

"You understand the terms of the agreement and the way the interest works, right?" Jezabel asked again. She knew she didn't have to, but she wanted to make sure the lady knew that even if she paid the loan back in a month, she would still owe the interest for longer than just the summer.

"I understand," the woman said. "I just have to get through this month, is all. Running out of important things and I just haven't had the money or the business, and the winter was so cold."

Jezabel heard this a lot, especially when winters were harsh. A utility bill for even a small house could rise over $500 a month easily. Jezabel knew all about that because her apartment ate a couple of hundred to heat, and she always tried to keep the temperature at about 68 so she would have some "fun" money left over. Then, sometimes Michael would come through and give her some cash, or he would take them somewhere fun, so she would save money that way, too.

Michael. Lately, whenever she thought of him, she had the same feeling she got when she looked at milkweeds in the fall, after all their fluff had gone to seed and started flying off. But she didn't want to consider that right now. And she sure as heck didn't want to be thinking about fans. She typed a little faster, hit the print button, and told the lady she would be right back.

In the lobby, Tonya picked up one phone line after another. Six or seven people sat in the cracking, plastic orange seats by the storefront window, and another three or four people vied for parking spaces out front. This was freaking ridiculous, Jezabel thought. She couldn't process all these people by herself. Even if Charles were here, they would still have people waiting.

But she had Tonya. A pretty black lady from this neighborhood, Tonya knew how to handle herself and others. That's why she was so good at her job. She wasn't afraid of more than one person coming in at a time. She could handle the rude ones, the impatient ones and the sneaky ones. She got them through intake, and if she thought there was something really suspicious about a client (other than the usual working-under-the-table, concealing a criminal record or hiding minor drug deals), she would make reference to her fiancé who was a cop and how excited she was that he would be coming in any minute now to have a cup of coffee with her.

The truth was, Tonya had been divorced from her retail-district-manager-husband for three years, didn't have a fiancé that was a cop or even a fiancé for that matter. Though she was well under thirty, Tonya said she was through with men. But she did legitimately know a couple of the cops from the station two doors down, and her tone was so convincing that no real, dangerous thug had ever called her bluff. It was amazing the way a truly shady character, after talking to Tonya, would suddenly get a cell phone call and have to come back at another time.

Tonya prided herself in this art of bluffing and subtle intimidation while still being polite, and she knew it was one reason Bobby and John would never even want to think about losing her as an employee. Jezabel was sure Tonya got paid very well. And she was sure that anyone who got by Tonya was not a violent scumbag — with the possible exceptions of Bobby and John themselves.

It seemed to be getting worse every day. Each morning, shortly after the doors opened, potential clients filed in. The seats filled up fast, and often, it was standing room only, with a wide array of people from every country represented in the microcosm that was the lobby of In-a-Pinch. And what they all had in common was a kind of poverty that relied on loans, these high interest loans supposed to provide a quick fix and a way out.

"Tonya, is Sharon coming in today?" Jezabel asked, though she knew she wouldn't like the answer either way.

"Yes, ma'am," Tonya replied.

Great, thought Jezabel as she grabbed her papers from the printers. Just great. Sharon-I'm-so-proud-to-be-working-in-the-financial-industry-Stuart.

Sharon wore a gray or navy blue suit every day, practical pumps and a pressed, white blouse. Jezabel couldn't tell if Sharon belonged on an airplane serving ginger ale or in Washington, D.C. serving papers. Sharon spoke clearly, enunciating every word as if articulation were a job qualification in this zoo.

"What time is she due in?" Jezabel asked.

"'Nother hour," Tonya answered.

"Okay. Please, just tell people I am alone until then and to hang on. It might awhile. They can get some coffee or come back in a couple of hours if they don't want to wait."

"Okay," Tonya said. "Whatever works for you. I'll keep 'em at bay."

Jezabel knew she would.

Tonya was such a good person to work with, so strong and polite at the same time, rare qualities in this industry, in fact, in any industry. She half wished Tonya had another job. Tonya would could work anywhere and make good money. She didn't have to rely on Bobby and John. She could go out and do something meaningful.

Jezabel wished she were in the same position.

Back in her office, Jezabel saw the red-haired, fan-fixing lady cleaning her globular glasses and pacing. "Okay, I just need a couple of signatures," Jezabel said sitting down at her desk. She was thinking about Michael and the park again. Stop it, she scolded herself. Focus.

The lady sat back down. "You know, your office is kind of stuffy," the lady said, taking a pen out of the penholder on Jezabel's desk. "You could use a fan in here. You can…"

Jezabel pointed to the places that required signatures. "Sign here and here," she interrupted. "Then I sign as a witness, and I can get you a copy for your records."

"So what do you think?" the lady asked. "About the fan, I mean."

This lady is relentless, Jezabel thought, but she was used to clients trying to sell her things. After all, that's what a good sales person did, and it put Jezabel a little at ease thinking the lady was ambitious and assertive.

"I think the owners won't approve the expenditure," Jezabel said.

"Well what about for your house? You have a house, right? You need a fan for your house? I can get you a fan for your house."

"Um…I have a good central AC system and a big fan. I'm all set. But thanks anyway," Jezabel said. Her voice was flatter than she meant it to be, but she needed to discourage the lady and still be gentle about it. Not that Sharon was ever gentle. Sharon was a stucco wall trying to pass herself off as 1970's velvet wallpaper.

"Well, if you ever need a fan, you know how to get in touch with me," said the lady. "Just call me. I can sell you a good fan, a really good fan, or I can fix one that broke or I can…"

Jezabel got up to make copies. "Excuse me," she said, going back to the lobby.

A trip to the copy machine was always an excellent escape. When she returned to her office, the woman was pacing again. Thinking the lady must go through a lot of footwear this way, Jezabel handed her the copies, shook her clammy hand and told her to have a nice day.

The woman smiled briefly and said, "Okay. Call me about that fan."

"I will if I need to," said Jezabel. And the woman walked out of her office, breaking into a tuneless whistle as if life had just given her something wonderful to look forward to. Jezabel wondered if fans made the woman happy. Was the woman happier than she was?

Jezabel drummed her fingers on her desk, a relic from the 1970's, evolved from cheap wood and scratches. She couldn't remember how many times she had listened to the sound of her nails against that wood as she waited for another client to come in. The sound was that noticeable no matter how brief.

Yes, that was her day and most of her life. Client after client. Then go home. Feed the cat. Talk to or see Michael. Call her mother once a week. That was about it. She should have been further on by now, or at least she thought she should have. She really did need to do something, needed more fresh air, maybe a walk outside when time permitted, if time ever did permit anything more. But time, like most other things in the world, wasn't very generous.

She considered the onslaught of incoming clients, damning Charles again. He had not worked here that long, a month or two at max. Maybe he didn't really want to work here. But it wasn't her concern. She didn't want to work here either, but she had to and she didn't want to be the only one processing applications. And she surely didn't want to have to play tag-team with Sharon.

"Jezabel, I would like you to meet…" Tonya's voice pinched Jezabel out of what was actually a ten-second reverie. "Jezabel is going to take care of you from here," Tonya said.

"Have a seat, sir," Jezabel said.

The client smelled expensive, freshly cologned. The black man, in a gray pinstriped suit, leaned awkwardly in the plastic chair. No one ever seemed comfortable in these chairs, which Bobby and John probably planned when they had chosen the chairs years ago.

The man's polished shoes looked out of place next to Jezabel's beat-up desk. Honestly, she didn't know why some of them had to come here at all. She felt pretty poor next to them.

But then, if anything, this job had taught her never to judge the client by the dress or the car or the cologne. Some of the best dressed people were the poorest, most hard-working people who had legitimately fallen on hard times and only had their clothes left to show they had ever done well in life. Or some were those who had over-borrowed and would always live on the edge of collections and repossession as a result. Still others shuffled in on canes, barely able to walk and afford their monthly medication costs, but looking stately somehow.

Of course, there were the gamblers, the players, the drug users and dealers who owed their superiors money, the ones who never seemed to learn that a quick fix wasn't the answer and neither was a life in the alleys and basements of the city. For some of them, this place had become a kind of financial addiction. They lived from loan to loan, like they did from game to game and fix to fix.

She took the papers he handed her and asked the usual questions. "You understand…" she began.

"Yeah, I understand," the man cut her off. "Just continue."

"Sorry," said Jezabel, glancing up at his face. "I have to remind you of that, legally."

"I know. Let's get on with it," he said.

She wondered why he had to take the loan. It couldn't be good, whatever it was, judging from his reaction. She processed the rest in silence, only indicating when she had to get up to retrieve the prints for him to sign. He signed quickly in small, neat, cursive letters. J. F. Frank. She noticed his name because the writing was so sophisticated looking, like him. She stared at her shoes. Flats. They weren't that old, but they weren't shiny like J. F. Frank's, either. Better off people would have tossed or donated shoes like hers.

By the time J.F. Frank left, Jezabel needed coffee. Back to the lobby. Tonya always understood the why's of Jezabel's mini-breaks and never begrudged her.

In-a-Pinch wasn't really a big place. Jezabel spent much of her day walking from her office to the lobby and then back, sometimes just to get respite from the walls that were strong enough to strangle a person, but mostly to pick up documents from the printer or make copies. The tiny bathroom at the rear of the building gave a contemporary meaning to the term "water closet" and provided a little escape. It smelled like mold and bad breath, so she went only when absolutely necessary. Bobby and John had other properties, bigger ones, but they would never waste those on the people or employees of In-a-Pinch. At least, that is what Jezabel assumed.

She rarely had time to leave for lunch. Sometimes Tonya asked Jezabel to cover the front while she ran out to pick up some food for everyone.

"Good afternoon, ladies, and how are we today?" Sharon asked as Jezabel stirred her coffee.

Sharon had entered the room like it was a fashion runway. She didn't just walk in. She announced her appearance in her smooth, articulate voice from a mouth that gave only the illusion of a smile. Jezabel didn't even pretend to smile back. Why pretend? She hated Sharon.

"Just fine," Tonya replied.

Tonya wasn't all that crazy about Sharon either, but Tonya was more used to faking smiles from working in the front. And Jezabel knew Tonya wouldn't want to give Sharon the satisfaction of knowing they had struggled, shorthanded this morning.

"You have Mr. and Mrs. Guadalupe here, waiting for you, Sharon."

Sharon nodded, her hair staying in place from what must have been expensive spray. Sharon was an expensive woman.

Jezabel pressed herself against the doorframe to get back into her office. She avoided brushing against Sharon, as if the woman had some kind of catching snob disease. Sharon made her exquisite exit, while Tonya made her confident one. Tonya brushed against Sharon on purpose, probably just to see if she could make Sharon flinch. Sharon prevailed, however.

A minute later, Tonya was introducing the next client, an elderly man with generic looking eyeglasses, a cane, and something stuck to his chin. Jezabel didn't want to stare to find out exactly what that something was. Maybe he had cut himself shaving. Maybe he had dripped something from his meager lunch. Stop it, Jezabel told herself. Stay focused.

"Well, I don't like doing this kind of thing," the man said, as he handed Jezabel his paperwork. "Seems just so expensive somehow but I just got to this point I kept falling behind and then the missus, well she needed those diabetes pills and even with the Medicare that put us behind. Gets harder and harder every day, seems like," he said.

Jezabel nodded. She understood more than he knew she did. "So I am thinking if I take this little loan, I can have it paid off in six months or so. See I have a couple of stocks. They aren't doing good right now, but in a couple of months, you know, things could change, and then we will be all set. But right now..."

She entered his information, nodding at him as he continued. She wanted to be kind, so she softened her tone as she reminded him what sort of loan he was getting. He sat closer, his cane parked firmly in the tile floor of her office, his head tilted as he listened intently.

"I understand, Miss," he said when she had finished. "Like I said, this is just for the time being. The missus, she's diabetic and needs that medication. I have high blood pressure myself and I stopped taking the medicine. Last time I saw the doc, he read me the riot act, I tell you. So I'll take this here little loan and get some of that medication for the both of us. But don't you worry. I always pay all my bills."

"I am sure you do, sir," Jezabel said. "Let me go make some copies for you to sign."

Jezabel could hear Sharon annunciating to her clients in the office across from the copier. "And you know, it is my duty to remind you that this is indeed..." Jezabel mouthed Sharon's speech, mimicking her, screwing up her face to the printer as she did so. "Bitch," she said silently.

God, that lady drove her nuts. Today she was wearing another navy suit. It looked like it was made of wool or something. Her shoes were spotless, and her blouse... Jezabel wondered how many of the same ones Sharon actually owned. She pictured a closet full of blue and gray suits, white blouses and sensible, expensive, new shoes. Barf.

"Here you are, sir," Jezabel said, returning to her own client.

He got up, leaned on the cane and took the copies. "Well, I thank you, young lady. I am sure I will not see you again, so you take good care of yourself."

"And you take care, too," Jezabel said. She felt like it was the most sincere thing she had said all day, and it struck her somehow as sad.

The day passed along one, interminable, bumpy road, client after client, listening to stories, saying the same things, wondering if it was time to leave, wondering if there were more to life and thinking there had to be another way for these people to get money. But that would put her out of a job. She wondered if she should start counting how many clients she served, the way Tonya logged the number of clients coming through the front door. Disgusted, she realized she even had the same kinds of thoughts, day in and day out. Nothing changed, ever.

At 5:00, Jezabel shut down her computer, mentally saying goodbye to her favorite photo of her and Michael in the park, put on her jacket, deposited the last bit of paperwork in Tonya's inbox to be filed, and walked toward the door.

"Is it time for you to leave already?" Sharon called from her office. "My, I just do not know how it gets to be this late. You are lucky to be leaving early," Sharon said.

"I get in at 8:30," Jezabel reminded her, immediately wanting to stifle herself. Why should she have to remind Sharon what hours she worked? Sharon wasn't her boss. It was none of her damned business. Just because Sharon worked the later shift didn't mean Jezabel was responsible for discussing their difference in schedules.

"Well it must be good to come in that early. You don't have as many clients first thing in the morning, I suspect, as I do in the evenings after they have all finished work for the day. That is when it starts to get very busy," Sharon said.

Jezabel nodded. Sharon had said this before. Jezebel literally bit her tongue, struggling not to remind Sharon of all the elderly and poor lined up before the doors even opened, and that unemployed people could come any time they wanted, which was usually during the day.

"And when Tonya leaves so early," Sharon continued.

Why was she doing this? Tonya didn't leave early at all. Tonya came in the same time Jezabel did. What the hell did Sharon care? "Are you worried about being here alone?" Jezabel asked, not out of concern, but with the intention to pepper Sharon with a little worry.

"Oh, no," Sharon said. "The security system is in place, and the police are so conveniently close."

Which is why Tonya used the police as a convenient way to deter violent criminals from requesting services. In-a-Pinch sat on the corner of Gorham and Essex, with the northern police station less than a block to the left of them. Cops passed by their windows all the time, stopping in the café across the street, now and then holding up traffic to let a pedestrian cross.

Tonya had an easy job of waving cheerfully through the front window and beckoning in the police to play "fiancé" whenever she needed it. And the cops, who shut their eyes to the nature of In-a-Pinch's business, were happy to play the part. Still, Sharon would not be so lucky. Who would want to even pretend to be Sharon's fiancé?

If traffic counted towards stats, the city was pretty busy, but it didn't offer as many jobs as people needed. It didn't even have as many stores as it used to. Houses had started to look more world weary. Streets and sidewalks had potholed pavement, and the lawsuits against the city had soared. And the way the recession was working lately, it didn't look like it would be getting better any sooner.

Jezabel was smart enough to know that a bad economy and high poverty rates secured her a job. But she was also smart enough not to question that too much. She didn't need to be feeling guilty about how she made her own ends barely meet, especially when she didn't feel like she had much of a choice.

"Well, you go on now," said Sharon. "I would not want to be the reason you had to leave late."

Jezabel pushed the door open, feeling the cold against the palm of her hand. Her feet hurt. Her shoes never felt right at the end of the day, like her feet had swelled throughout the hours she sat at the desk.

The walk to the bus stop would not be pleasant today. It was March, and March was still a little more than chilly. The wind had died down, leaving the memory of cold, as the dull orange sun dissolved behind the early evening clouds. This kind of chill usually deterred her from taking a walk or doing anything requiring extended time in the mean outside eager to inflict a head cold.

At her apartment, Jezabel had wanted to turn the heat off and just use her electric blanket at night, but so far, that was just a want. The cold won. She didn't want to test fate and get herself sick. While she had some sick time, she didn't have enough to cover, say, the flu. And besides, the owners of In-a-Pinch frowned on employees taking sick time even when it was necessary. Not that Charles seemed to care.

Cheap bastards, Jezabel thought. They were the kind of owners who pretended they treated their employees well, throwing little Christmas parties in the lobby, giving out cards and boxes of Whitman's chocolates for Valentine's Day, but when it came down to it, Bobby and John Spellini could care less about their employees or clients. They cared about profit.

They wore Armani suits into Dunkin Donuts. All the old men drinking coffee and reading the newspapers would put down their cups, stop and stare. It was hard to tell if the stares were generated from awe or disgust, but either way, the Spellinis got the attention they were looking for from the people they wanted to attract. There were some people — like police detectives — the Spellinis did not want to attract, and they usually didn't. Local cops couldn't really touch them, nor did most of the cops have any desire to. After one or two failed attempts to nail the Spellinis, the Chief had called a kind of truce, so long as the clients were peaceful and laws were seemingly followed.

Bobby drove a 1968, fully restored, flaming red Corvette. John drove a new, black BMW. They both wore wedding bands and, in their wallets, kept pictures of their perfectly manicured wives. Jezabel knew both men regularly cheated on those perfectly manicured wives. She did her best to avoid or ignore the owners whenever they happened to visit. And she certainly averted her eyes at the obvious mistresses who sometimes came in with their lecherous lovers. At least those lovers didn't try to slum it with the employees or clients.

The thing that set Bobby and John (and Jezabel always alphabetized their names, for some reason) apart from other thugs was that they gave to charities — not a lot of money, but enough to make them look like good, churchgoing folks. They attended Catholic Mass every Sunday, sat in one of the first few pews and bowed their heads when the priest prompted the congregation in the Act of Contrition. They even went to confession every Friday. Were they confirmed in the church, Jezabel wondered? Who would confirm these guys? Who would serve Holy Communion to Bobby and John when the more traditional priests would deny Communion to anyone they knew had openly committed a mortal sin?

Enough about Bobby and John, Jezabel thought. Leave them at work or in whatever dark alley they inhabited after hours.

She was the only one at the bus stop, and for that, she was thankful. Wisps of her blond hair blew in ribbons across her eye, and she shook her head, irritated, looking for the bus and wanting it to show soon. She had a car, but it had a bad habit of breaking down. Besides, at work, there was nowhere to park except in the street, and the last thing she needed was to have her ten-year-old coupe hit or towed or stolen. She didn't want to have to fight her clients for parking, either. It didn't seem right somehow, and the effort would not be worth it. Might just as well take the bus and help the planet.

The bus finally trembled into sight, squeaking Jezabel's thoughts out of her mind, veering towards the sidewalk, the door opening to reveal several empty seats.

Thank God. She wasn't into hanging from the bus poles like a monkey the way she used to do as a kid. It had been fun then, but it wasn't now.

She didn't remember being this tired as a child. Life was new then, like the stuffed kitty she had received on her seventh birthday, the kitty she still kept on her pillow. Her own kitty loved to snuggle with the fake.

She clinked some tokens into the old style, metal collection box and headed back to the last empty seat she could find. The vibration of the bus, the feel of the wheels, the squeak of the shocks as it moved on the road, making turns, slowing, stopping, letting on other passengers, letting some off, soothed her in a strange way once she had settled comfortably into her seat. It was a time when she could let go, let someone else do the driving, let someone else be in charge, make the decisions and collect tokens. For twenty minutes, she could look out a window and think about nothing, the landscape of the city streaming by in a colorful band of buildings and cars and people and streetlights brightening against the dimming day.

The stop was less than a minute away from her apartment, a basement unit three doors down from the laundry room. It was an okay place, she thought, turning the key in the hollow wooden door. It wasn't a big complex, fairly quiet. There weren't many break-ins, so the cheap door and almost useless doorknob lock rarely worried her. Besides, Michael was around some of the time, so it wasn't like she was totally alone. She knew he wouldn't be there tonight, though, because it was Monday, and he liked to watch football at his place with his buddy on Monday.

Tony was Michael's closest friend in and out of work, and she guessed Monday was something Tony looked forward to as much as Michael did. A buff-looking Italian guy with an easy smile, Tony had a sweet, pretty, dark-haired girlfriend named Jen, someone Jezabel liked but didn't know much. The two couples got together once in awhile, but usually, it was like tonight—boys' night.

Just as well. Jezabel wanted the night to herself, wanted to absently read a cheap novel and turn in early with her two cats, the real one and the stuffed one.

Tarika greeted her at the door, rubbing herself against Jezabel's leg, exhaling a meow that made Jezabel feel guilty about having only one real cat. Truthfully, she thought about getting another one to keep this long-haired, black and orange-striped fur ball company during the day, but Michael already complained about Tarika, and if they ever did move in together like they talked about, the cat thing would become an issue.

Jezabel wouldn't want to give up Tarika, but she didn't know if she would if she were given the tough decision to make. She and

Tarika had been together for five years, she and Michael for three. Never mind. Don't think about it, she told herself, scratching Tarika behind the ears.

"Hi Baby Girl," she said. "You hungry?" Tarika purred steady as a windup clock and headed to her food bowl. If anything, Tarika loved to eat. And Jezabel loved to listen to Tarika's purrs.

Jezabel looked at the answering machine. Nothing blinking. No messages slipped under the door, not even an ad. She was too tired to check regular mail and email (probably junk and spam anyway), so she opened a can of diet soda and flopped on her couch, watching Tarika dive head first into the bowl of fishy smelling kitty chow.

The purring and grunting reminded Jezabel of a pig eating from a trough. She laughed silently. Maybe she would rename Tarika "Gip," "Pig" spelled backwards.

Boy. She was getting more than just a little pathetic, sitting here with her cat, laughing at her own jokes. There simply had to be more than this, no matter how much she loved her cat. When would she get more out of her job, out of her life, even out of her relationship? Again, she squelched the thoughts. Be happy with what you have, because you could have less than your clients, she reminded herself.

"Huh?" she said. "Who? Michael?" Jezabel mumbled into the phone. "What time is it? What are you doing?"

"Well I just thought you needed a call, baby," he said into her ear.

She scrubbed at her eyes with sleepy fingers. What time was it?

"What? Don't you want to hear from me? Don't you miss me?"

"Yeah, I miss you, Michael," she said finally waking up enough to comprehend. "What're you doing?"

"Finishing up with my buds here."

"You working tomorrow?"

"Not me, baby. Ground's still froze where we need to be tomorrow."

Michael worked construction off and on. Sometimes he worked with Tony, but not always. Tony had a second job, telemarketing to subsidize during the winter. Jezabel wished Michael would do the same, but he most likely wouldn't be very good at it with his brusque manner.

When the work was there, Michael made good money, but

it was inconsistent, and he wasn't very good at saving. There were times when Michael couldn't pay his own rent and Jezabel gave him an advance that always seemed to turn into a permanent loan. She didn't have Bobby and John as collections backup, and she wouldn't want it anyway, considering her feelings for Michael. Inconvenient, she thought, because it put her on an even tighter budget.

"So I got to party hardy tonight."

"Where'd you get the money to party?" she murmured, her eyes scanning for the clock.

It was 2:15 in the morning.

"What's it to you, huh?" he asked. Then he chuckled, "Come on now. You know I have to have my Mondays."

"Yeah, I know. Listen, Michael, I have to get some sleep. I have work in the morning."

"Oh, you saying that to make me feel bad?"

His tone changed. He could go hot to cold pretty quickly when he drank too much, but she was used to it. When he was just buzzed, he was friendly and lovable as Tarika. When he got drunk, he could be all-out mean.

"No, hon, I'm just tired is all," she said. "Okay?" She hoped it would pacify him. Sometimes when he got like this, he didn't want to hang up.

He wanted to argue. He wanted to goad her. She would fall for it occasionally, but not tonight, in spite of her crappy day, one that would have made most people take the bait.

Once when he was like this, she tried to just hang up on him, but he came over to her apartment and banged on the door until she opened it. She didn't want to think about that night again, or she wouldn't get any sleep.

"Okay?" she said again. "How about tomorrow night you come over and I'll cook us a nice pot roast. I'll use the crock pot, like you like it. Sound good?"

He paused. "Yeah, whatever, okay," he said. And he hung up.

She inhaled, pulled the covers up to her ears and rolled over. Tarika purred against the back of her legs, and Jezabel was thankful for the fur and purr.

Chapter Two

Maurice and Stella both sat facing the desk, not looking at one another. Maurice had a fat, white stomach coated with coarse, dark hair, the curly belly-bristles threatening to pounce from the bottom of his t-shirt that read, "If you don't like my attitude, don't talk to me." He tapped his thick, black work boot impatiently on the tile floor and stared openly at Jezabel as she entered their information into the system.

"How do you intend to pay this loan?" Jezabel asked flatly, suffocating a yawn.

She was exhausted. After the call from Michael, she couldn't fall back to sleep, and when she did, she kept dreaming that same dream she always had, that she was five and falling off her beloved, shiny, red two-wheeler, over the sidewalk which happened to lead to a gully which rolled off to a steep hill surrounded by jagged rocks and the white water of the same canal running through the city. She never could seem to recover from that dream and after an hour or so, decided to make some coffee, read National Geographic Magazine, and finally, get dressed for work.

No problem. She was here, wasn't she? And these people's paperwork didn't exactly need her full attention when she had done this so often. Pink goes to them. Yellow goes to the file. White goes up front. Sign the disclaimer first, the one she had to read to them aloud.

Jezabel thought if the stupid disclaimer was that important, the Spellini brothers should have it enlarged and framed and hang it in the lobby over Tonya's desk. But maybe if the poor souls in the waiting room read that disclaimer again and again while waiting for their turn to dig their own economic graves, they might turn around and head out the door. Then again, maybe not. Desperation does terrible things to people.

Stella snapped her gum. "We're going to sell some more trunks on eBay," she said in a strong accent that Jezabel thought screamed New York, Boston or both. Or was it New Jersey? Jezabel couldn't tell with some people. Could even be Rhode Island.

"We have three of them sitting in the cellar waiting for him," she thumbed accusingly at her husband, "to get off his rear and finish them. When he does, we will be all set." She reloaded her gum for another bubble shot.

Jezabel glanced at the woman. Hadn't she seen this couple on a sitcom somewhere? Most of Stella's brown roots streaked through the blond. She wore a large gold watch with rhinestones around the face and a thick gold necklace chain Jezabel suspected were real gold. Stella's mouth was lined with some kind of plum cosmetic, and her lipstick had worn off, giving her face the look of a clown that needed a touch-up. Her skin had that look of someone who smoked and spent too much time in the sun, but there was something kind of endearing about her smile that Jezabel wasn't consciously aware of. Somehow, this woman was likeable, in spite of herself.

"Well if you wouldn't buy so damned many of those trunks, maybe I could get to some of my tools down there and get it done, but the way you have it now, I can't hardly get into the cellar," Maurice shouted, jerking to face his wife, his fists clenched.

"Cripes, how the hell am I even supposed to get to the sander, huh? You got it all blocked off with the trunks and clothes and stupid-assed little trinkets and crap. It's fucking ridiculous."

Jezabel looked at him sharply, continuing to type. "Sir, I have to remind you this is a place of business and foul language will not be tolerated."

It wasn't the first time she'd had to say this, so the words slipped smoothly off Jezabel's tongue even though her mind stumbled over "place of business." She wanted to add, "such as it is."

"Oh sure, you too, huh, siding with her just cause she's a woman," he said, sitting back against his seat and starting to tap the floor again. "Fine. I get it. Just keep doing your job. I'll stay out of it."

He had used that tone Jezabel recognized, the one sometimes used by insulted, bullying men, the one meant to inflict a guilt trip but rarely worked on women like Stella. It often worked on people like Jezabel, however, no matter how often she ranted and raved in her head.

Maurice scowled at his wife and then at Jezabel.

"Now I have to remind you that this is a high-interest loan that must be paid..."

"Yeah, yeah, we know. We've done this before. Just get on with it," Maurice snapped.

"Sir, I'm sorry, but I have to say this, legally," Jezabel said and continued reciting the disclaimer.

"I will be right back with your copies."

Jezabel could hear them revive the argument as she went up front. Just another day in Paradise, she thought.

Sharon was at the copier, and Jezabel could hear Charles' usual stage whisper, spouting off the disclaimer to his clients. At least he was in today, and Jezabel wouldn't be stuck with Sharon and a bunch of clients all by herself with just Tonya functioning as front-line protection.

Charles was a pain, but he did have a decent sense of humor, which was much more than Jezabel could say for Sharon, or even for herself most days. Besides, he had a way with people—at least the people who weren't too down or crippled to smile—that made him invaluable in ways other than just keeping up with the lines. Which was probably why Bobby and John had hired him.

She grimaced, accusing herself of relating to her clients far too much and too often lately. She thought if she could just get herself to do one thing differently, alter the pattern in just some small way, maybe that would be what she needed to change direction. But she didn't know what that one thing was, didn't have enough time or imagination to think it through, and frankly, didn't have enough motivation. Her exhaustion was inspired by more than just lack of sleep.

Maybe she should take her shoes off. Maybe that would do something.

"I'm all done," Sharon announced, stepping aside to let Jezabel at the copier.

"It's all set up for two-sided copying. I know that is what you will need to do with those contracts," Sharon pronounced.

Whatever, lady, Jezabel thought. Like I don't know how to copy by now. Besides, who the hell cares, Sharon? Single-sided, double-sided, why don't you go work for the freaking government and get out of my sight?

"I think it confuses clients when we make single-sided copies," Sharon continued, ignoring Jezabel's ignoring her. "They have a difficult enough time understanding what we are trying to communicate, and when we use more paper than we have to..."

She just went on and on, her mouth moving with nothing but bureaucratic diarrhea spilling out.

"When I see either Mr. Spellini, I am going to recommend we have the settings on the machine locked. It will increase productivity and lower overhead. And..."

"Don't you have a client waiting?" Jezabel asked. Sharon paused and blinked at her.

Jezabel took her own copies back to the lovebirds in her office.

At the moment, they were giving each other the silent treatment, each with arms folded, each looking in opposite directions.

"I have copies for both of you to sign on the two lines below," Jezabel instructed.

"You go first," Stella told her husband.

"No," he said sarcastically. "You first. Really. I insist."

"Maurice, just sign the damn papers so we can get outta here and you can get to work."

"Oh, and I suppose that's your way of saying I'm a bum?"

Oh my God, thought Jezebel, here we go again.

She cleared her throat and handed the pen to Stella. "Ma'am your line is here at the bottom. If you would sign..."

"See that?" demanded Stella, signing on the line, "Even she doesn't want to deal with you. Total strangers can tell. No one wants to..."

Jezabel tuned her out and handed the paper and pen to Maurice. He grunted, signed and handed the pen and copies back to Jezabel.

"Here are your copies," Jezabel said, giving them each a set and keeping her own. "If you have any questions, the office number is at the bottom of the page. Have a nice day."

She moved to sit back at her desk. She began typing again. Both of them just stared at her. She looked up. "You can leave now," she said. And with that, Stella nodded and walked out. Maurice tapped the floor three more times, got up with a huff and stomped through the door.

Jezabel wondered if he would stomp all the way to the car, and if she counted his stomps, if she would reach over fifty. Never mind. Too depressing and not nearly amusing enough to get her through today. She would rather picture his stomping, tripping on his bootlace, and landing face first onto his wife who would have to decide to either catch him or step to the side. Which one would Stella choose, Jezabel wondered?

"Yo, Jezzy, what you doing?" Charles called from his office. He was obviously fully recovered.

"Just the entry parts," she called back.

"Aren't you even going to ask how I'm feeling?"

"How are you feeling, Charles?"

"Much better, thank you for asking. You know how those viruses are. Bad stuff going around."

Liar, Jezabel thought. He could at least have the dignity of pretending he had been legitimately sick.

"Yeah, I bet," she said. "I know all about those viruses. Who gave you yours, Charles?"

He ignored her question. "What you doing for lunch?" This was typical Charles, asking about lunch at ten in the morning.

"Don't know yet," she said. "Don't know if I have time."

"Aw come on. You can buy," he called.

"Not me. I go, you pay."

"Excuse me," Sharon raised her even tone to one that could obviously be heard throughout the offices. "I am trying to complete this paperwork."

Her emphasis fell on the "k" of "paperwork."

"It can be difficult to concentrate when there are other conversations going on. Would you mind going into each others' offices if you have the time and need to talk?"

Charles poked his head into Jezabel's door, mouthing Sharon's words, mimicking her inflections. It was one of the things that made it easier for Jezabel to tolerate Charles's poor work ethic — his dislike of Sharon and his sense of humor made up for some of the nastiness in the office.

"Ladies and Gentlemen," he said, raising his voice an octave and annunciating quietly, "The Captain has turned on the 'no smoking' sign. Please fasten your seatbelts and remain seated until..."

Jezabel allowed herself to raise one side of her mouth. Yes, he was immature, unprofessional and unreliable. But at least Charles made her smile.

She shook her head. "You better get back into your seat before the grand dame reports you."

He stuck his tongue out. "I ain't doing another thing before I refill my coffee cup." He sauntered off to the front.

Jezabel wished she could be as cocky about her work as he was. Or was it that he just didn't care and could afford not to care?

On his way back from the coffee maker, Charles reported there were three people waiting for Tonya to do intakes. The phone rang.

"Thank you for calling In-a-Pinch. This is Jezabel McPhearson," she said.

A male voice imitated hers: "Thank you for calling...this is Jezabel McPhearson."

"Hi Michael."

She was pleased he had called her. Sometimes, they would go a whole day without getting time to talk, and that didn't feel right to Jezabel.

"Do you want to do lunch?" he asked.

"Oh!" she said. She felt that nice, cool sensation of surprise slip up her spine.

Usually if he wasn't working, Michael would spend the day relaxing in front of television or maybe getting some grocery shopping done. Going out to lunch spontaneously like this meant something. In this case, she hoped it meant he had gotten paid and was in a better mood than last night.

"Sure. Where do you want to go?"

"I don't know. Subway is right across from you. Let's do that."

"Okay," she said. "I can get off at noon."

The sub shop was the regular place Tonya or Jezabel would run out to when they picked up lunch for each other. It was convenient, and what would make it special today was being there with Michael.

"Kay. See you then."

Jezabel smiled. Michael wasn't the most romantic figure, and lunch at Subway wouldn't be the highlight of most people's lives, but for her, it was enough of a switch, a step away from routine to get her thinking maybe this was the little change she needed to get out of her rut, her funk. And she wouldn't have to take her shoes off to do it.

"So seriously," Charles said, coming back into her office and sitting in one of the client's chairs. "What are you doing for lunch?"

"Michael called. I'm meeting him," she said.

"Oh...Michael," Charles teased. "Going to meet your little boy toy. I understand."

"He's not my 'boy toy,'" Jezabel laughed. "He's my significant other."

"Oh, even better!" Charles laughed, slapping his knee. "Your significant other! You've been listening to Sharon for too long!" he guffawed. "Oh shit, that's funny. Your significant other. I haven't heard that term in a long time..."

"Jezabel," Tonya's voice interrupted them as she walked in, and Tonya gave Charles the "get out of here" look she reserved just for him. "This is Ms. ..."

"I know," Charles said. "I know. You don't have to look at me like that more than once, woman. I'm leaving."

"Well good," Tonya said, "cause I'm bringing your client in right after."

"Have a seat," Jezabel said to her client. She was still smiling, and the young Hispanic woman smiled back at her. Jezabel didn't usually smile at clients, but she decided not to break up the pleasant rhythm of the one she had going on her face right now.

This girl was different somehow. Or maybe it was Jezabel who was different.

"Let me take a look at your paperwork," Jezabel said.

The girl—and to Jezabel, she seemed like a girl in her late teens—just smiled. She smelled like mashed potatoes and fruity hair spray, a nice mix somehow. Her dark hair was long and straight, and she looked oddly excited to be here in spite of whatever reason had brought her in.

"How do you intend to pay this loan?" Jezabel asked.

"I do lot of work," the girl said. "I clean and babysit and on Saturdays, I work at the movies. I sell tickets. I make good money."

"Okay, but you are taking out this loan. Why?" Jezabel asked.

"I want to buy nice present for my mother," she said. "For her birthday."

"Oh."

Jezabel stopped. She looked at the girl, so ready to pay more than she had to, so willing to work as many hours as it took, just to buy a present for her mother.

It made her sad, and she thought about her own mother, living far away, and what they did on birthdays. They called each other and sent each other gift cards to Wal-Mart. Jezabel didn't really have the option of working overtime or sending her mother special things because…why? She thought for a minute. What would happen if she did try to send her mother something special, something out of the ordinary, something different?

She shook the thought away, remembering the last time she had tried such a thing. She had bought her mother a leather bound new translation Bible, had it wrapped and sent express for her birthday. Her mother called that day, left a message that she read only the King James version, that she had returned it and gotten a gift card that she would send to Jezabel's aunt in Iowa. Jezabel didn't try to send anything different or special after that.

"Is…that okay?" the girl asked, looking at Jezabel's expression.

"Oh, no, it's fine," said Jezabel. "I was just thinking, is all."

She entered the information into the system and found herself wanting to hurry out to get copies. The room felt stuffy now, and the scent of potatoes and fruit didn't strike Jezabel as pleasant anymore.

She moved her mind in a different direction. Maybe Michael would walk in the park again with her some time soon. They needed a new picture taken together. She remembered how they had taken the first one, the one that was on her computer screen. On that gorgeous, colorful and mild day, an old couple walking hand in hand had made their way down the same path she and Michael did. They smiled at her and Michael in that "how cute" way older couples sometimes give younger ones, and Jezabel had smiled back.

The man had noticed the camera swinging from Jezabel's

hand and asked if they wanted a picture together. Snap. There it was, trapped in digital and emotional memory. Jezabel wondered if the couple knew how long that picture would last, how she would put it somewhere to remind her every day of that day, and how it had become one of her favorite memories.

Back to her office in a better mood, Jezabel recited the disclaimer, realizing how moody she had become over the past few months. Was she turning manic-depressive?

"Okay, I need to remind you that In-a-Pinch is not a bank. You are taking out a high interest loan to be repaid over a six-month period. You will be responsible for the principal of the loan, monthly interest accrued at 27% and the initiation fee of $75.00. If you miss one or more payments, we reserve the right to aggressively collect from you and/or the cosigners designated on your application form. Do you have any questions?"

The girl nodded. Jezabel might have wondered how much the girl really did understand, but she had worked with people like this before. They always paid on time. They would do whatever it took to get this loan off their hard working backs. She could tell this about the girl without talking to her extensively. After all, anyone who worked three jobs and took out a loan to give a gift to her mother...

By the time the girl had signed and left, Jezabel was more than ready for lunch.

Michael was late. Jezabel kept looking at the gold-tone face of her watch strapped to her narrow wrist by a thin, cracking, black leather strap. She had only a half hour to eat, and if Michael was late, well then, that would take up a good portion of that little time she had. She doubted Bobby or John would ever come by to check up, but she and they knew they didn't have to. They had trained her well.

She also knew how Sharon was, and she knew Sharon would be the first one to write down and report anyone tardy, even if it hardly ever happened. It was just the kind of person Sharon was. Once, when Tonya was late, Jezabel found a post-it note stuck to the keyboard of Tonya's computer. Sharon came by and quickly plucked it away, frowning at Jezabel, but not before Jezabel read, "9:20 and Tonya still is not here." Jezabel never trusted Sharon, but this confirmed it was more than just paranoia.

Michael strode in fifteen minutes late. She could tell it was him even as he approached the door. His green and orange jock jacket made him stand out somewhat in a crowd, his work boots streaking caked on clay and mud as it fell off in clumps across the restaurant store even though he hadn't worked that day.

Hands in his pocket, a lopsided grin across his good-looking face, his dark beard hid whatever other expression accompanied the grin.

Sometimes, Jezabel wished Michael were uglier. It might have made her worry less about him finding someone else, or it might have motivated her to consider why she worried at all and encourage her to re-think their relationship. And even if she had no intention of leaving him, it would have made it easier for her to fight back when they had an argument.

She wondered if Michael felt the same way about her, wondered if he found her good looking as well as sexually attractive in the same way she saw him. But if he did, Michael never seemed daunted by her looks when they argued.

Still, she and Michael had been together for more than five years now, and that had to count for something. They had created a history together. Michael had his bad habits, to be sure, but Jezabel knew every one of his bad habits. There was no way she could tell that if she took the leap toward someone else, that someone else wouldn't have habits worse than Michael's. It wasn't a gamble she wanted to take, or at least she wasn't ready to take it right now, no matter how much things irritated her at times. She could still list Michael as one of her favorite things.

"Hey," he said, sliding into the bench.

"Hey. I ordered you a steak and cheese," she said, pointing to the sub and drink at his place. "I only have another fifteen minutes left. I thought you would be here earlier. I hope your sandwich isn't soggy."

"Yeah, well, I got a call at the last minute. Got a job coming up next week."

"Well that's good, isn't it?" she asked.

She didn't want to sound too happy, or he would question whether or not she believed he could get a job. Also, she never knew if the offer was a decent one.

That was another trick. If Michael accepted one job lasting a week or two, there was always the chance he would have to say no to a better proposition with a higher bid for a longer time period.

"Not bad," he shrugged, unwrapping his sub and taking a bite.

He talked with his mouth full.

"Kind of a crapshoot. It's half done, so won't matter if the ground is frozen. It's out a little bit far, but should be okay. And they might want an outbuilding after, so it could be longer term."

Jezabel nodded.

For the umpteenth time, Jezabel wished Michael would learn

to save more when business was good. Maybe then his off-seasons wouldn't be so difficult.

Like some kind of bad Déjà vu, Michael cleared his throat and said, "I was wondering if I could get a little loan until I get some money coming in."

She looked at her sub, listening to Michael finish chewing and take a sip of his soda.

Jezabel hated this. He knew how tight money was for her, especially with the high utility bills at her own place. She was annoyed he would ask her again for a loan (this would be the third over the course of the winter), but she understood. She worked all day long with people who didn't have enough money, and the last thing she wanted was for him to look for that money at a place like In-a-Pinch. But then, what did he expect her to do? She had her own rent to pay.

"So whaddya think?" he asked her, now taking a big gulp of the soda.

"I don't know, Michael, I have to see how much I have. I haven't paid rent for the month or anything yet. And I just had to pay that huge gas bill."

"Oh," he said.

She looked up. He was frowning. "Well, if that's how it is…"

"No, no," she said. "It's not that. I just don't know how much I have. Let me go home and look at the account and I'll let you know, okay?"

"Okay," he said and took another big bite of sub.

Jezabel was waiting for the inevitable, his suggestion that they move in together. He had suggested this several times, especially lately, arguing for it mostly during the winter months when he said it didn't make sense for them to be paying for two apartments when they could easily share and cut their expenses in half. Jezabel understood the economic aspect for sure, reminding him that she did work in a financial institution, no matter how sleazy it was, but just didn't feel ready to make that kind of leap. He looked at it as a step rather than a leap and didn't understand what her problem was.

Truth be told, he scared her when he started talking like this, especially because immediately after, he would go down the road of having kids. Michael really wanted kids. He wanted them as soon as possible. The problem was, he didn't seem to care if he and Jezabel got married that fast. He didn't see marriage as having much to do with having kids.

Jezabel didn't relish the idea of raising kids with Michael as her boyfriend and not her husband, and neither of them with solid careers. She really didn't want to consider her work at In-a-Pinch a career, no matter how much she felt stuck.

"Of course, we could solve this and just move in together," he chewed. "Like I've been saying."

There it was, as she'd predicted.

"Michael, we have talked about this before," she said.

"Yeah, and so how about it? We've been together for awhile."

"Michael, I don't know. I just think..." She looked at her watch. "Oh my God! I have to go!"

"Yeah," he said. "How convenient."

He slurped at the bottom of his soda.

"No, really. Listen, Michael, I'll give it some thought. I mean some real thought. Then I'll look at my account and let you know, okay?"

"Sure," he said. "Whatever."

"Don't whatever me," she said, coming around to kiss him. "Thanks for meeting me for lunch."

He offered her his cheek. "Yup," he said. "No prob."

She walked back into the cold air, and he sat, continuing to eat, his back toward her. She didn't look over her shoulder to see if he was looking back at her, trying to give her a wave or blow her a kiss, the way he used to whenever they had to part.

Sharon was lurking in the lobby when Jezabel came through the front door. The irritating woman wore her best, fake smile and Jezabel looked at the clock. She wanted to hit herself again. Why did she look at the clock? She knew she was on time. Why did she let Sharon get to her and make her second guess herself?

Who cares, she thought. For the first time this week, there was no one waiting in the waiting (had poverty taken a lunch break, too?), and Tonya was just coming back from the restroom. There was no sign or sound of Charles, so Jezabel assumed that meant he was still at lunch. Charles didn't care an ounce what Sharon did or said about his work habits. Let her report him. He said he hoped he would get fired. Then he could collect unemployment.

Jezabel walked back into her office, listening to Tonya tell Sharon she was all set and didn't need her to watch the front anymore. "Are you sure?" asked Sharon sweetly. "It's easy, so if you need another minute or so..."

"No thank you," said Tonya, firmly, and Sharon's footsteps sounded closer as she went back to her own office.

Jezabel was interrupted by Tonya and the next client, a neat-looking man in his early forties. He wore dress pants, a button-down shirt and a tie. His leather jacket, unzipped, looked newly treated. It was shiny, and the leather smelled fresh, as did his breath. He wore his hair closely cropped, and his clean shave looked like it had been done that morning. Jezabel would have guessed he worked as an insurance company owner or a software developer. What he was doing here? She didn't even want to guess because it would just make her worry more about the economy and other things she could not control.

"Have a seat," she said, indicating the chair.

She was more aware of the tacky furniture, the scratches on her desk and the general feel of the office whenever someone who looked like a member of the middle or wealthier class came in. Like with her other suited client, the environment just didn't match this guy. The man didn't seem phased, however. He simply handed her his application.

"I see you are self employed," she said. "What industry?"

"I'd rather not say."

She paused, looking up at him to see if he was smiling. He wasn't.

She didn't know quite how to respond. This was a new one on her — usually Tonya screened out anyone who came off as genuinely shady.

Jezabel scribbled "contractor" in the "industry" field. As soon as she could, she turned her chair and started entering the information into the system.

"Does it matter?" he asked suddenly as she typed.

"Well, there is a question here that asks it. I just put you under the 'contractor' heading, but there will be other questions later that I will need answers to."

"That's fine," the man said. "All you need to know is I can pay the loan back."

He sat with his hands in his jacket pockets, looking around Jezabel's office like he was assessing it. She wished he would stop. She knew the walls hadn't been painted in years, and scratches and fingerprints dulled the appearance of the finish. The florescent lighting only drew more attention to the ugliness of the office, in spite of the small floral prints Jezabel had hung in the middle of the far wall to break up the depression of dirty-white. She suddenly felt like her surroundings and her job represented her.

"I need to ask how you plan to pay off the loan, sir," Jezabel said, wishing she didn't have to. She knew he would be resistant.

"I will pay it off with my next paycheck," the man said. "That will be in exactly two weeks." The man's voice was crisp, not unfriendly, but succinct.

"Um, I'm sorry, sir, but I need to know what you will do for work to pay off this loan," she said.

"You already asked what business I am in, and it's general," he said, irritated.

"I know, but they need to know specifically what you will do to pay this off, even if your line of work is general business. I'm sorry. I don't make the rules. And I know it's kind of like asking the same question twice. I think it's some law or something."

"I'm a consultant," the man said, now through thin lips. "You can tell them I'm a business consultant."

"Okay," she said, now really curious why he needed this loan when he obviously had a regular paying job, albeit one he didn't want to discuss. Maybe he owed his bookie or something. But then, it could be he just got in over his head or his wife or girlfriend wanted jewelry or he had a gap in employment like Michael.

Maybe his girlfriend was like Michael and asked to borrow money, which made him…

Stop it, Jezabel, she reprimanded herself. Pay attention. Stop daydreaming and trying to figure out things that don't concern you.

"I'll be right back with copies for you to sign," she said. The man nodded.

"Hey Tonya," Jezabel said, nearing the copier. It was still pretty slow this afternoon. "Have a good lunch?"

"Yeah," Tonya said, "until I came back to the Queen Mother hovering over my desk, acting like the place would fall down without her incredible powers of oversight."

Tonya wasn't particularly quiet. Jezabel knew Tonya got as aggravated with Sharon as she and Charles did, but for some reason, no one ever said anything about it so loudly. In that way, Tonya didn't care. She had more stability than perhaps anyone else in the office.

Still, the assumption was that Sharon had some kind of special relationship with Bobby and/or John Spellini. No one thought Sharon was sleeping with either of them—she wasn't half as good looking as the owners' wives or the owners' parade of borrowed women— nor did she seem like some kind of exciting conversationalist the two playboys would enjoy. But there was something there that prevented the three others from officially complaining about Sharon in spite of Tonya's assertiveness.

"I know,' Jezabel said. "Hang in there."

Jezabel made copies and returned to her mystery client.

She handed him his paperwork, and he signed before she could say a word.

"Sir, I have to remind you," she began.

"I know," he said. "It's the law, and it's your job. Go ahead."

Jezabel wondered again about this man. Apparently, he had

done this before. Why? And again, why did she care?

She began, making extra sure she enunciated every key word of the disclaimer, wanting to sound at least a little intelligent. Oh my God, I must sound just like Sharon, she thought between sentences.

"You are taking out a high interest loan to be repaid over a six-month period. You will be responsible for the principal of the loan, monthly interest accrued at 27% and the initiation fee of $75.00. If you miss one or more payments, we reserve the right to aggressively collect from you and/or the cosigners designated…"

Jezabel had to comfort herself again that this man had been screened by competent Tonya and that probably, he could pay, and that probably, he was not an ax murderer.

Then it hit her, right in the middle of her speech. She kept talking, but she understood something that had been lurking at the edge of her mind, something she had tried to fence off.

It had to do with Michael. She would look at him and worry about his job situation and his money problems and her money problems and then look at professionals and think certainly, a clean-cut guy with a shirt and tie or a well-dressed man with cologne and shiny shoes could do better than come here. She knew, intellectually, when it all came down to it, that it didn't matter what kind of job you had or what you wore to work. That work could end in a second and land you up here, a shabby office signing away your life to the likes of Bobby and John Spellini. It was a conundrum.

But she sometimes wished Michael were more of that perfect, middle-class person, the one in the tie, the one with the steady income, the one with manners, the one who would have unemployment and disability and health benefits, someone who would never consider turning to In-a-Pinch or to a significant other for a loan.

Maybe with a little help, he could become that person. Maybe it would just take a little more teamwork to make it happen.

She knew then what she was planning to do when she got home.

Chapter Three

She couldn't believe she had done it. Staring at the telephone, she thought about the conversation. Less than five minutes. That's all. She almost laughed at how ridiculous it was, how she could change her life in less than five minutes, as much time as it took to request cable television or order a full course meal.

"Well, I decided you were right about us living in separate places," she had told him. "I've been thinking about it. It doesn't make sense, what we're doing, especially when you stay at my place most weekends already. I mean, what's a few extra days? It's like we live together already anyway, isn't it?"

"Yeah. That's what I've been trying to tell you," he said. He sounded genuinely pleased.

"So, what do you think?" Her heart had been beating so frantically, she thought she could hear it bouncing against the phone.

"Yeah, it's cool," he said.

She hadn't wanted to say anything else, waiting for something more from him besides that initial reaction. Didn't he want a timeline or something? To talk about the logistics? To discuss Tarika?

"So can you give me that loan?" he had asked.

She had been taken off guard, like being knocked down while keeping close watch on a princess locked in a castle tower.

"Well, um, you know…I wasn't really even thinking about that. I thought if we did this thing, you wouldn't need the money."

"Nope. I still need it. Needed it three days ago," he chuckled.

"Oh."

"You don't want to? Okay. Hey, I understand. I'll figure it out. Go pawn something."

He knew she hated it when he talked like that.

"No, no, it's just that I still didn't even look at my checkbook or bills. I was just so focused on making this decision is all."

"Well give me a call back when you look," he had said.

That was it.

What had she expected? Some kind of romantic outburst from

him? Appreciation or thankfulness? Why would he do that when they were just talking money sense? Besides, like they both were saying, he spent most weekends at her place anyway. And again, she had made the decision and she had told him. She had taken care of it. The loan was just one more detail before they could solidify their plans. It was good. It really was.

She wondered if Michael had maintained a better relationship with his parents if things would be different. As it stood, he had alienated them years ago when he had started taking drugs and landed himself in a gutter. Since then, they hadn't trusted him with money, though they offered him a place to live if he went into rehab. He had been too stubborn.

Michael literally hit bottom the day he went to work. He was high and fell off the roof of, thankfully, a one-story home. He then used his stubbornness to kick the drugs right in the face. Jezabel had been attracted to his self determination. No everyone could overcome a drug habit, especially on their own.

Had he been as stubborn about his career as he had been then, both he and Jezabel would be in a different place. But she worried she might not have been in that place with him. Right now, they were on a pretty equal economic footing, in spite of the loan issues. It was always hard on a relationship when one person earned significantly more than another, even if one turned housewife or househusband. Jezabel never wanted to feel dependent even if she worked in other, non-paying ways. And she certainly couldn't imagine Michael as a househusband.

She put her head against the back of her tweed couch. The rough texture bit at the back of her neck, and she was suddenly conscious of how old the couches were, and again, how tired she was. She thought about taking a little nap right there, then thought about how the only place she had ever been able to sleep was in her bed, and then thought about the living arrangements again. They both had queen size beds. Michael would want to keep his. She would want to keep hers. How the heck could this possibly work out? She guessed she could give up her spare room to Michael's bed. It might be nice to have a guest room for the first time in her life, not that she knew who she could invite over, other than Tony and Jen.

Taking her panic out on her tongue, she bit down hard, then went to her second bedroom and turned on her computer. The same picture she had on her computer wallpaper at work lived on her own computer. She took a good, hard look at it and decided to smile. Blue skies. The park.

Maybe tomorrow, she would get off at the earlier bus stop

and walk there herself, loll in the memories and the future she had to look forward to.

The image of Michael and her holding hands followed her to her bank account balance online. If she put off paying the electric for two weeks and paid less on her credit card, she could give Michael the loan and pay the electric the day before it was due. She didn't like to do that, but it was an option.

She picked up the phone. He didn't answer. He's probably in the bathroom or something, she thought, and left a message. "Hi hon," she said. She didn't often call him that, but tonight, she felt like she could and should somehow. "I have enough for the loan. Give me a call back." She hung up the phone.

She decided she did need a nap after all.

She awoke to the feeling of numb feet and the telephone ringing. What time was it? What was wrong with her feet? "Hello?"

"Hey babe," Michael said. She smiled, remembering her decision, and thinking about how he wouldn't be calling her like this anymore. He wouldn't have to. He could just roll over and...

What time was it? How long had she been asleep?

Her eyes found the clock. Midnight. And the cat had been asleep on her feet, making her feet fall asleep as well. A full-body sleep, just what she needed.

She tried to focus in on Michael's conversation. He was telling her about the stuff he was going to sell before they did this big move and getting more to the point, when could she get him the money? Could she do cash? It would save a lot of time so he wouldn't have to run to the bank. He added that selling furniture would give them a few extra dollars, maybe even the same amount of the loan. Jezabel was doubtful, considering the condition of Michael's furniture, but she didn't want to discuss it at midnight and maybe never at all.

"Sure, hon," she said. "Cash is fine. I'll get it tomorrow night and when you come over, you can have it."

It was Friday, thank God. The end of the week. By tomorrow night, she would have survived another week of Sharon's condescending behavior, Charles' outrageous talk, Bobby and John's nerve-wracking possible visits and the constant flow of need that came and went through her office door. Friday night, and a weekend with Michael. She could survive just about anything.

"You want to see that new movie on Saturday night and go out for a drink or something? Celebrate?" she said.

"Sounds good," he said. He laughed. "You're paying, right?"

"Yeah, I'll put it on the charge." She was feeling good after her nap, a bit frivolous, in fact. "Wish it was the weekend right now," she said a little lower into the phone.

"Will be soon," he said. She could hear his smile through the wire, and she loved his smile. "Get some sleep. See you tomorrow night."

She hung up and realized she had slept through dinner. She was starving. Not one to eat late at night, she padded through the dark apartment to the kitchen. The refrigerator light shone through the night, and a small beam from the streetlight filtered through her living room window. String cheese and yogurt and a glass of apple juice. That was fine.

She hoped living together would make both Michael and her eat better. She grinned into the dark, thinking about coming home and cooking meals for the both of them, Michael turning up his nose at her new inventions and asking, "What the hell is this?" He did that now sometimes, on weekends. It would be fun to do it all through the week, she thought.

She ate her snack on the scratchy couch, looking out the window. The streetlights made it impossible to see stars, and the flow of traffic past her apartment window made a hum she hardly even heard anymore, she was so used to it. But the view comforted her, probably more so than the couch.

She remembered her move here, about five or six years ago. When her mother had decided to leave, and Jezabel was just in college. Jezabel had been living in the dorm and didn't know where she would go. She didn't want to find a place on her own at that time. She hadn't been prepared. She had been planning on going back home in the summer, working and saving some money. Now that wasn't an option. Mom had used the book of Proverbs to justify her decision. "Train up a child in the way he should go; even when he is old he will not depart from it," she quoted. "I've trained you right. You'll be fine."

So Mom moved, and Jezabel stayed in the dorm for another term until she decided college was not for her. She just couldn't get into it, the huge lecture halls, the room with three other roommates, the business major that didn't seem to offer much more of a future than she thought she could get on her own. She landed her job shortly after, got her apartment and quit school for good.

The job and apartment felt so new and exciting then, especially the apartment. The walls were freshly painted. The rug smelled like fibers, the way new rugs did. She had nothing really to put into her place except for the few things she had brought from her dorm. She slept on a blow-up mattress for a week or so. With her first paycheck, she bought a set of dishes, silverware, drinking glasses and more blankets. She bought some groceries, a few cheap cooking pans and napkins. Then, she went to the thrift store and got a real bed and a small kitchen set. The furniture was beat up, but she didn't care. She could use scratch remover and polish it. It was hers. That was all that mattered. And she amazed herself how she could do all this and still pay her rent.

Each month, Jezabel bought some more trappings to make a comfortable home. She was nesting, using scraps, balancing on economically precarious, leafless branches.

Not long after moving in, she had met Michael. On one of their first dates, he helped her pick out a used television, noting it wasn't as good as his, but it would do for now. She hadn't bought cable, which he complained about, but she said she didn't watch much television. She did buy a used DVD player, so when he visited, they could watch a rented movie.

That felt like a long time ago, and in the context of her age, it was. Michael didn't start staying at her place until about a year after they met. But Jezabel was happy. Now, she had her job and a boyfriend and an apartment. The third-hand car she financed wasn't so great, but hey. She would have it paid off in a year, and she could take the bus whenever she wanted.

Early on, she decided to get a cat even though the cost might prove burdensome. She adopted Tarika from the local shelter, and it was like the furry thing had lived there all its life. She remembered all the kittens clawing at the bars of their cages, the meowing and feline begging and the way Tarika, already four years old, just stood and looked into her eyes. There was a connection, thick as Tarika's beautiful coat.

Jezabel loved that cat. It was her cat. Michael instantly disliked Tarika, and Tarika him. He would kick the cat out of bed, and the cat hissed at him. Even now, when Michael came through the door, Tarika would run and hide. Jezabel wondered if that was how it would continue, if the Tarika would hide, or if they would get used to each other. Michael hadn't even mentioned the cat, so that was good. Maybe he was just all talk about really hating her. Some people were like that.

Jezabel finished her snack, went to her room, changed, and slipped back into bed. Tarika had been keeping it warm for her. Jezabel gave her a goodnight pet and fell instantly asleep.

"Jezzy, Jezzy, Jezzy," Charles said, shaking his head as

Jezabel hung up her coat. He was sitting in one of her client seats, drumming her desk with a couple of pencils. "Oh, you better watch out," he chanted. "You better watch out or Sharon the lady will make sure you are out." He wrapped it up with a complicated drum scheme that included beating the metal edging of the chair next to him.

"Thanks, Charles, that's just lovely," she said, sitting down to her computer. "But I hardly think they will fire me for being ten minutes late once a year."

"Well you just never know," he said, grinning. "Could be your lucky day. Me and you, baby, in the unemployment line..."

She had to laugh. Charles was a trip.

"Yeah, I heard you laugh," he said, proud of himself. "You ain't laughed enough lately there, Jezzy girl. What's up with that?"

She paused. Maybe it has been more noticeable than she thought. "Things were getting boring," she said lamely.

"And now they're not?" he asked.

She freed a giggle and then covered her mouth, embarrassed. What was wrong with her? Charles grinned, waiting.

"Michael is moving in with me," she said quickly, like she was afraid if she waited any longer, it either wouldn't be true or she wouldn't say it.

"Uh oh!" Charles said, the smile slipping from his face. "Are you serious?"

"Yes, I'm serious! Why wouldn't I be?"

"Well, this is an awful big step, you know," he said. "Wouldn't catch me letting my girl move in with me. Too much crappola. You sure you want this?"

"Yes," she said, and then caught herself wondering. Stop it, she told herself. Charles is just trying to freak you out is all. He's probably just jealous. Besides, he didn't even have a girl.

The truth was, she always did wonder if Charles was kind of jealous of Michael. Charles liked to come in and chat with Jezabel quite a bit, and sometimes he would bring her lunch and things to drink. At first, she thought he was just being friendly, but then one day, Tonya started teasing her about Charles being Jezabel's other boyfriend and did Michael know? Jezabel told her to shut up, that Charles was just friendly. "Uh huh," Tonya had said. "You keep talking, girl. Maybe you'll believe it."

Jezabel wanted to believe it because it made it easier to have fun just talking to Charles. When he chose to come in, of course. He was funny. He wasn't the most professional employee on the planet, but Jezabel didn't care about that, especially considering In-a-Pinch wasn't the most professional place on Earth. Charles could make the day go by a little faster and alleviate the lines a bit. She appreciated that about him. It wasn't romantic. It was friendly. She liked it. And she did resent when he called in sick.

Once, Michael came in, and Charles was sitting in Jezabel's office. Charles stood up, introduced himself, shook Michael's hand. Michael just grunted. Jezabel, embarrassed, excused herself, leaving the two alone, which was probably the worst thing she could have done. When she and Michael were outside, he let her have it.

"What'd you do that for?" he demanded. "Leaving me in there with that clown. Who the hell is that guy anyway? Where's he from?"

"I guess he's from around here," Jezabel said. "I don't really know."

"Looking like he does, he ain't from around her," Michael said. "Don't ever do that again. You want me hanging around your freaky foreign friends, you warn me first at least."

"He's not foreign," Jezabel had said. "He's…"

What had Charles said?

His mother was Jamaican and his father was Portuguese—that was it.

Charles had an interesting look about him. He was tall and thick but not heavy. His skin was the color of dark maple, and he had long eyelashes. He always seemed to wear the face of a wise-assed, grinning, high school kid, but he wasn't at all malicious. Sometimes there was the faintest hint of a Jamaican accent in certain words he used, but other than that, Charles spoke what Jezabel had heard termed "light street-wise." And he was proud of his name. He never let people call him "Charlie" or "Chuck."

"So you really gonna do it, huh?" Charles said, tugging her mind back to the office where she would prefer not to be. "Uh, uh, uh," he said, shaking his head. He held out his hand to her. "Allow me to express my deepest condolences. I'll buy you the sympathy card later."

"Shut up!" she said laughing, slapping his hand away. "It's going to be good. Besides, it'll be so much cheaper than what we're doing now. Right now, we're both struggling, so this will really help."

She wasn't sure why she felt she had to justify this to Charles or why she was suddenly spilling her finances to him. Not a good move if he happened to turn on her and repeat it to Sharon who would love this juicy morsel of potential blackmail. But somehow, she couldn't picture Charles turning on anyone, and she really couldn't imagine him dripping information into Sharon's gossip I.V. tube.

Tonya walked in with a client for Jezabel. "I'm sorry to

interrupt your meeting," she said mocking seriousness, "but may I introduce your next client…"

Charles bowed elaborately and took leave. The Asian man Tonya had been escorting sat down. He was holding his papers on his lap, looking straight at Jezabel.

"Thanks, Tonya," Jezabel said. "How are you this morning, sir? Can I have your application please?"

The man just looked at her. "Sorry?" he said in a thick accent.

"Your application?" she asked again. She pointed to his packet. "Your papers?"

"Ah, okay, here my papers."

Like she did with other clients, Jezabel wondered and almost worried how much English the man knew. He obviously knew enough to come in here, but that didn't necessarily mean he understood everything from the intake, the application, or the brochures. As she entered his information, she asked him, "So how are you today?"

"Excuse me?" he said.

She looked at him and said a little bit more slowly, "How are you?" She didn't want to sound condescending.

"Ah, good, good," he said smiling and nodding.

Thank God.

She smiled back.

He was cute in his own little way, neat twill pants and a mulberry colored checkered, button-down shirt, tie shoes, looking kind of like a school boy but with more charm.

"You understand the information?" she asked slowly. He cocked his head. Uh oh, she thought. "Um…you understand the papers?"

"Papers? You need more paper?"

"No, no," she said, shaking her head. "Do you know what this says?" she asked even more slowly, pointing to the papers. "Can you read this?" He looked at her blankly. She tried again. "You read English?"

"Ah! Yes, yes, I read," he said. "Talking not so good. Reading, better." He grinned proudly.

She nodded and smiled again. Whew. At least he knew what he was signing, to some extent.

"Okay," she said, the typing done. "I be right back."

Stupid. Why was it whenever someone had a thick accent or dropped their verbs, after listening to them talk, she would pick up on it and start talking like them? It was really embarrassing. What if he thought she was making fun of him? She wasn't. How could she explain that?

Luckily, he hadn't seemed to notice. Instead, he was looking around her office, whistling so quietly, she mostly knew it by the form of his mouth and not the sound coming out. He looked content. She would have liked to be content like that, calmly making decisions and then just letting them play out however they would. But that wasn't how she was built. She would think things out. Yes, she would think them out again and again for a long time. She would plan and she would figure. And then she would make the decision. But even though it was a conscious decision, she would always go back and second-guess herself, just like she was doing now about the impending move-in.

She hated when she did that, second-guessed herself. If anyone else went through a similar decision making process, she would tell them, "Well, you did all your homework. There is nothing else you can do to plan, so don't be so hard on yourself. We can't control everything in life." So why did she expect something more from herself? It wasn't a logical part of her personality. And Jezabel really did try to be logical.

Oh no. Speaking of illogical, Jezabel thought. There was Sharon. Sharon, in all her gray-glory today. "Ladies and gentlemen, the color of today is gray," Jezabel thought, picturing a game show host speaking quietly into a microphone, giving the audience a hint that the contestants weren't privy to.

Jezabel took the plunge. After last night, she was feeling brave: "Good morning, Sharon," she said.

"Why good morning, Jezabel. And how are you today?"

"Just fine. Looks like another busy day."

"Well it sure does," Sharon said, raising a neatly penciled eyebrow and donning a fake smile.

Jezabel saw Charles's head poke abruptly through his office door. He looked incredulously at Jezabel and mouthed the words, "What the fuck?" Jezabel stifled a laugh. Two surprises for Charles today. First Michael, and now Sharon. It was, indeed, a fun kind of day.

Back in her office, her client was still softly whistling.

"Okay, sir," Jezabel said. The man stood up and offered her his hand in a goodbye.

"No, not, not yet," she laughed, and motioned for him to sit.

"Ah, I sorry," he apologized and sat down.

Here we go again, she thought.

"Okay. I must say this," she said slowly. "This is a high interest loan. You understand high interest?"

"Yes, yes, high interest," he repeated.

"Okay, good. This is a high interest loan that you must pay back. How will you pay this back?"

He tilted his head.

Let's try again, Jezabel thought. "Do you work?" she asked.

"Yes, I work," he said. "I work hard. I count."

"You...count?" Jezabel asked.

"Yes, yes, I count and I give numbers to store. They sell things."

"Oh!" said Jezabel. "You are an accountant?"

"No, I not accountant," he said. "I just count. Manager. He accountant. I just count."

He started to laugh, and for some reason, she found it hilarious and started laughing with him. The more she laughed, the harder he laughed, and before she knew it, tears were streaming in a clear, steady line, and the man was slapping his knee.

"Oh!" he said, gasping for breath. "Funny...I not accountant. He accountant. I just count!" and he laughed all over again.

Then, Charles did come in. "Am I missing something this morning? Jezzy, what is in your coffee, girl? I ain't never seen you like this!"

She tried to explain through her laughing mouth.The man took out a handkerchief and wiped his eyes.

"He said he counted and I thought that meant he was an accountant but really, what he does is count and give the information to the store accountant.

"And that's funny...why?" Charles asked.

"Oh never mind," she said, wiping at her own eyes. "I can't explain it."

She giggled a couple more times. "Would you excuse us now or I will never get through the disclaimer," she said.

Charles just shook his head and walked out. "Strange-o." he muttered. "Never can understand women."

"Okay, now enough of that!" she pretended to scold the man.

He pretended to look apologetic. "I sorry," he said.

"So you work and you pay loan," she said. "And since you count, you understand loan?"

Dammit. She did it again, talking like he talked. She went on quickly. "You pay interest. If you don't pay, they make you pay. Do you understand?"

"Yes, I understand," he said. "No problem me paying. I pay just fine."

"Wonderful," she said. "I need you to sign here and here." She handed him the pen. He found the signature lines and signed in small, neat handwriting.

"Your copies," she said, giving them to him.

"Thank you," he said. "I all done now?"

"All done," she said.

"Wonderful!" he said. Was he imitating her now? "Thank you very much."

"Thank you, sir," she said, extending her hand. "You have a great day."

"You have great day, too," he said, and smiling once more, walked out.

Jezabel hummed as she entered his information into the computer. She couldn't remember the last time she'd had fun with a client like that, and over what? Some stupid joke that she couldn't even explain? Maybe she was just giddy. That had to be it. Giddy and stupid.

In the next moment, she decided she had better revert back to her old self. Sharon was knocking politely at her door, even though Jezabel's door was always open. "Everything okay in here?" Sharon asked in pseudo-innocence.

"Yes, fine, why?" Jezabel asked.

Damn. Shouldn't have asked a question. That gave Sharon a reason to answer and talk to her longer.

"Oh, I just thought I heard a disruption is all," she said smoothly, pronouncing each syllable. "I thought perhaps a client was giving you a difficult time, and we don't want that, now."

"No, I'm fine," Jezabel said.

She wanted to say, "I was laughing with a client. You ever do that Sharon? Ever laugh with a client? Ever laugh at all?" But she bit her tongue, which was getting a bit sore by now, and just typed until Sharon understood that she was dismissed.

"Well if you ever need help or a client gets out of hand, you just let me know, now, okay?"

"Sure, Sharon," Jezabel said.

Sharon was the last person Jezabel would call. Tonya would be the first, Charles the second. Tonya would throw the idiot out. Charles would laugh him or her out.

Sharon back in her own domain for the moment, Jezabel took her brief trip to the lobby to drop off copies and get another cup of coffee.

Tonya was directing a red-headed girl in a blue hospital uniform through the application. "No, you need to fill in your current income here, even if it's nothing," Tonya said. "I know you work. But not everyone does, so just fill in what you make here," Tonya repeated, getting irritated. "No, not after taxes. 'Gross' means before taxes. Here. Take the clipboard and have a seat." The girl sat down looking sad and confused.

Tonya got up abruptly and joined Jezabel at the coffee maker.

"Damn," she muttered so the clients couldn't hear. "No wonder they're here for this shit-assed loan. Can't even read the damned application. You think they have any idea what a rip-off this is? And this chick works at a hospital. That is scary shit, now, isn't it?"

"I don't think many of them do understand, no," Jezabel admitted.

Jezabel was surprised that Tonya had said something like this, considering how good she was at her job and how she obviously was rewarded for it by the owners. It was the first time she had heard Tonya mention the rip-off aspect of the business, and she wished Tonya hadn't done it at that particular moment. Jezabel was in too good a mood to start questioning the ethics of the place that kept food on her table, even if it was a table from a thrift shop.

"Unbelievable," Tonya muttered. "It's like I've never seen it before, all these clients, lately. Anyway…she's going to Sharon. Maybe she'll understand her better. Cause she sure as hell doesn't understand me!"

"Hopefully," Jezabel said, and she returned to her own office with some relief and a cup of coffee. Tonya, thought Jezabel. She sure is one tough cookie sometimes.

Chapter Four

She hadn't been near the park in so long, she almost forgot what stop to get off on. What was the name of it?

"Approaching Felonias Park," the bus driver bellowed back.

Yes, that was it. Felonias Park.

The driver was one of the few drivers that passengers could understand or hear, and Jezabel wondered if he bellowed to keep himself awake. She appreciated that and the fact he had reminded her of her stop's name as well as the name of her destination.

The bus braked abruptly at the corner, and she held onto the bar, jerking forward, barely escaping bumping the back of the gray sweatshirt in front of her, a thick figure of a man who smelled like suede even though he didn't seem to be wearing any. She hadn't been so lucky today — no seats left. But it didn't bother her so much because she didn't feel as tired as she usually did, she had laughed a lot and she had Michael on her happy mind.

She excused herself around suede-man and descended the stairs, the voice of the driver bellowing, "Have a good day."

"You too," she said automatically but sincerely. Did he hear her?

The doors squeaked closed behind her, yanking at the back end of her coat from the suck of the vacuum. She heard, rather than saw, the bus pull away from the curb.

It wasn't crowded on this corner. One or two people sitting in the shelter which was smoky glassed and carved up with initials and cuss words. That was it.

The city was funny. There were parts of it that never seemed to have many people on the sidewalks, and then there were places where you could barely find a space to call your own as you tried to make your way to the next corner. This wasn't one of those places. This was a quiet section with rows of authentic Victorian houses turned into apartments or offices. It wasn't fashionable, it wasn't popular and it didn't even have a street sign. If someone asked Jezabel what street her little park was on, she wouldn't be able to answer. It didn't matter.

Her feet knew the way.

The fence ran on her left as she made her way down the sidewalk. It was old-fashioned looking, cast iron with spikes on the end of each piece, painted black, a bit peeling, the kind of fence you might see around a cemetery or a haunted house. She thought of horror movies in which a hundred victims were impaled on such fences, and then she laughed to herself at the morbid thought making a cameo appearance among her other happy thoughts.

There was nothing scary or gruesome here. The sun was bright, the air was cold, and she couldn't wait to see the entrance, a sign on an arch made of the same metal design: Felonias Park. She didn't know who Felonias was, but whoever it was, he or she deserved thanks for keeping the little place separate from the rest of the city.

She looked forward as she passed under the arch. The walkway stretched in front of her, a length of cement through a sitting area guarded by cast iron benches on either side. Once past the benches, the walkway branched to the right and to the left, and it continued straight as well. Jezabel had walked all the routes of the park in all seasons, but the last time she was here, it was a rainy November day and too cold to stay long.

The fountains on the main walkway had frozen up and were shut down for the winter, puddles paralyzed at the bottom. The holiday lights, still up this March day, were ready to shine at night, a few winter decorations hanging in coniferous trees, but since the park didn't receive that many winter visitors, not many reminders of a holiday had been there or remained. The cold of the severe winter had kept her out until now, and today, with the birth of something new impending, she thought a walk here would make for a great, late afternoon.

She took the right walkway, eschewing a dead, stiff sparrow almost as naked as the bare oak trees. Some relentless crows, daring the cold, loitered about the branches, cawing at her as she passed. A squirrel or two scuttled over still-frozen grass, and she walked quickly. She wasn't cold yet — her coat was long, her strides long and her gloves thick. The purple scarf pulled around her ears kept her lobes protected from the mouse trap strength of the March wind. She didn't mind the cold, so long as she had winter clothes and kept moving. It wasn't like trying to get to sleep in a cold apartment or walking in bone-chilling rain. Besides, it was soothing to be here alone.

At this point, there wasn't much else to see in the park except for some short bushes, more benches, and off to the side, a larger body of frozen water. The pond was really a recess that tended to fill with rainwater and melting snow, so sometimes it nearly reached the edge of the sidewalk, but other times, it was completely dry. Now, sparrows, their feathers puffed up against the wind, convened atop the ice in the sunniest spots to absorb whatever the light had to offer.

A hundred more yards and Jezabel reached what she fondly remembered as "her woods." A group of trees with thick undergrowth at least an acre wide ran to the right of this section of the walkway. She and Michael had explored the woods before, she collecting acorns and pinecones for a holiday wreath.

At the time, she had noticed hoof prints or something in the dirt and wondered if any animals actually lived here or if something left over from the natural world was just passing through. For all she knew, it was just a big dog or a police horse.

She did eventually make her wreath, buying the looped branches from the local grocery store, adding the cones with twist-ties and carefully hot-gluing the acorns to the pungent pinecones and needles. A white bow completed the thing, and she hung it on the hollow wooden door of her apartment. She loved that wreath and wished it had lasted longer.

Now, it was still winter as far as the woods were concerned, and a thin layer of crusted snow remained on the floor, random pieces of grass poking through where the more frozen sections had broken into chunks of thick ice that reminded Jezabel of pictures she had seen of Antarctica and icebergs and the sinking Titanic. Part of a pathetic chicken wire fence ran alongside the woods, and Jezabel stopped a moment, peering through the clusters of heartier trees.

She thought of the picture on her computer again and remembered that day. The kaleidoscope of fall had prodded the city to look at the day through a lens, and it felt so good to hold Michael's hand and roam with him, walk in sync with him.

Michael had been telling her about his plan to build his own house, a place made to his exact specifications, a huge bathroom with a Jacuzzi tub and separate shower, the shower with ten showerheads set to high, massaging pressure. He told Jezabel how good she would look in his shower, and she had grinned, turning red, pleased that he thought of her intimately in his home, the home he was going to make.

His moving in was not quite the image she had pictured that day, but it was a start. After all, how would he be able to build his dream home without money, and what better way to save money than to have them move in together?

She remembered their conversation again last night and wished it had been longer. Was she imagining things, or was Michael pleased but not so excited about this move as she was? Or maybe she was just so nervous that she had to talk and talk and he had already made up his mind it was a good thing, so he had little to say.

She didn't like to push Michael to talk when he didn't want to. It sometimes put him in a bad mood. So she had hung up and decided to wait for him to express more of how he was feeling. Besides, they both had the loan to think about. This weekend, she thought. They would have time to discuss and plan more this weekend.

A rustle in the branches turned her full attention to the woods in front of her. Squirrels, two of them, played chase from one tree to another, leaping faster and faster, higher and higher like contending trapeze artists. Jezabel envied their balance and speed, and they looked like they were having such fun.

That's what she wanted to be in her next life — a squirrel in Felonias Park. The place was loaded with food, offered plenty of places to roam, had few enough visitors and housed ample squirrel friends to keep her company. She wondered if any horses had been through recently.

She turned back to the path. Jezabel could see the arch of the park entranceway. She pictured in her mind's eye the walk back to her lonely apartment, the strangers she would pass, the cars. She remembered that her mother was far away, and suddenly, without wanting to, she turned a little sad.

It sometimes seemed that loneliness just kind of ran in her blood. She had never known her dad, and she was an only child. She didn't have any friends except the ones at work, and they were more work friends than anything else. Michael had friends like Tony, but even though she liked Tony, he wasn't her friend. How long had she lived here and not really made any close friends?

Of course, Michael was her friend, but she didn't really count him because he was her boyfriend.

She remembered the first time she saw him. He seemed so tall to her. He didn't feel that tall any more. Wasn't that strange, the way some people could physically feel different once you got to know them?

He had been in the Dunkin Donuts, apparently drinking coffee before starting a new job. She was getting donuts for the office. He looked at her, and she had blushed because he had caught her looking at him. He grinned in that arrogant way he had, and she had paid quickly and rushed out.

The next day, she went back to the donut shop, this time for a coffee for herself. She'd had a lousy night's sleep and needed more than just In-a-Pinch's caffeine to get her through the morning.

He was there again.

This time, she made sure she didn't look at him. She stared at the menu, as if she would be tested on it later. She didn't know if he was looking at her, and she told herself it didn't matter, either. Who cares if some self-centered jerk knows I am looking at him or not, she remembered thinking. She had the feeling he was looking, though, probably trying to see if she was looking back at him.

The next day, she avoided the coffee shop, and the next as well. But then Tonya asked her to get her some "good" coffee the next morning, so Jezabel felt like she had to go.

Michael was there, but this time, she let herself look for just a second to see if he was looking. He was. She immediately turned to the floor, as if she had spotted some interesting insect.

He came over and started to put sugar in his coffee, stirring slowly, obviously staring at her now in that way that made her wonder if she should run the other way. She didn't run. She looked up. He was smiling at her, so she smiled shyly back.

And that's how it began.

He asked her if she came in a lot for coffee and she said yes, that she worked close by. She had wanted to say, "But you know that because you have seen me here before and that's a stupid line," but she didn't have the guts to. So he asked her if she wanted to come in a little earlier in the morning and have coffee with him.

She couldn't believe she had said yes to a stranger.

Those were the days when he would get up early and do things. He was motivated then. He went out of his way to get to know her and buy her coffee and donuts even when, she figured out, he didn't have a lot of money.

The walk in Felonias Park marked one of their first big dates.

Prior to that day, she had never been to the park, even though it was a lovely little treasure right near her house. Funny she didn't know about it until after she met Michael, but he had lived in the city longer than she had. She thought of it as Kismet and felt special that he had given her a gift besides coffee—another place to relax and enjoy wildflowers and birds after a long day of dealing with Sharon and sad clients.

Later that meaningful day, she showed Michael where she lived, and he stayed late into the evening. They actually talked and drank coffee, and Jezabel made him a tuna fish sandwich.

The next day after work, he picked her up, saving her from hanging on poles in the bus, and she went to his place across town. The apartment, sans curtains and a floor dressed in what she assumed was dirty laundry, rather startled her at first, but after talking to Tonya, she began to understand that many bachelors without lady visitors lived this way.

Then, one weekend, he came to her house and stayed a night. The following weekend, he asked her to stay at his place. Then he started staying at her place all weekend.

That's how it worked. He began to enjoy staying at her place more often because it was so much neater than his. She noticed the more he slept at her place, the messier his place seemed when she went back there. She wondered if he just decided he didn't need to clean up as much because he would be at her apartment, and he no longer had to keep his apartment clean so as not to offend her, or if he just had less time to wash clothes.

Still, she didn't mind him coming to her apartment on weekends. They had some good times, even if they just sat around watching television together.

She grew accustomed to Michael's Monday night football parties and now wondered what would happen to football night. She supposed many of the festivities would take place in her living room. That might make for some fun evenings.

Jezabel hoped Tony and Jen would start visiting more often, especially on weekends. She could picture having couples nights, double dates and intimate dinners. She was excited to talk to the couple about the move. Tony, an easy going character, was a native of the area, as was Jen. Both of them made Jezabel feel she fit in. She might get some close friends after all.

From further behind the tree line came another rustling sound, this one louder, like something bigger about to come through. This was curious. She had never seen a person out this way before. Once in awhile, she would see a little rabbit, and certainly chipmunks loved to live in the logs, but otherwise, she didn't think there would be...

She went in, just a little down a barely visible trail.

The rustle came again, this time closer. Jezabel froze, not because she was cold, but because she was listening.

It stopped, as if the animal had copied Jezabel.

She slowly peered into the woods, beyond the squirrels, beyond a couple of fallen pines. Farther in, she could make out a large rock and a cluster of bushes surrounded by a tangle of dried vine and fern that Jezabel thought must be lovely in warmer weather. She made a promise to herself to actually walk through this woods once the weather got nicer. But what was that she kept hearing?

Just beyond the rock, the tree limbs parted, like something starting to birth. But it wasn't just the lower limbs. The limbs over the rock as well opened like leafy doors, and then the middle of the trees by the rock did the same.

She couldn't imagine even a deer would be that big. Maybe it was someone riding a tractor or something, a caretaker? Or someone riding a horse? No, that was stupid. She didn't hear any machinery. And it was winter. Who would ride a horse in the city in the winter? A cop? Still, it sounded like something slowly approaching.

The outline of what she construed was a brown, hoofed leg stepped into the light of the rock. It was a big hoof, not like that of a deer at all, more like that of a Clydesdale or something. Had someone's horse slipped it reins and bits and run off to the park?

A second hoof stepped forward, and Jezabel followed the hoof up the leg as far as she could. The brown fur ended at what looked to be the underbelly of a creature, the rest of it still into trees and brush.

When the rest of the animal did appear, Jezabel wondered what she would do. In fact, she wondered if she should be standing here at all. What if the thing was rabid and decided to charge at her? Stupid, she thought. Who ever heard of a mad horse? It was the cows that had gone mad, not the horses, and the cows were only dangerous if you ate them. She had no intention of eating anything right now.

The thing took another step forward. The chest came through this time, and part of the back and then part of the body closer to the rear quarter. Still, no head was showing, as if the thing had its neck turned in the other direction, possibly feeding on something behind it. Or maybe it was eluding the idiot staring in its direction.

The branches rustled a little more consistently now, like someone moving through a clothesline of dried silk and linen. What was it eating? What did horses eat in winter, anyway, she wondered. It wasn't like there were carrots growing here in the park. She didn't have any sugar in her pocket, though she did, for some reason, have a packet of artificial sweetener from Dunkin Donuts. She doubted saccharine would appeal to anything other than self-destructive humans. She herself never touched the stuff.

Then, as far as it had come out, it retreated, back through the leaves. Jezabel cocked her head like a dog, listening. She stayed like that until her neck hurt.

Then, her head started to ache as a memory tapped on her brain.

The move. The loan. Oh my God. The account. The money. Hadn't Michael needed the money in cash? What was she thinking? She started to jog as much as she could in her uncomfortable shoes.

Here she was wandering around the city looking at imaginary creatures — because the farther she walked from the park, the more she was convinced she had imagined it or just wasn't seeing correctly —

when he needed cash. He was not going to be happy.

She took a quick detour through another section of the park, leading her to the block and bank. The ATM. She withdrew $200 and looked at her watch. How had it gotten so late? In another few minutes, it would be dark. She didn't want to be out here in the dark, and she didn't relish the idea of driving to his place in the dark if she could help it, but at this point, she didn't think she could help it.

She wondered if she had gas in the car. The last month or so, she hadn't really driven it because she had been using the bus, Michael was staying at her place, and they hadn't done anything requiring travel. He left his rickety truck at home, but it didn't matter because they mostly stayed in and watched television, called out for pizza, and fooled around.

The car. That was something they would have to address. Neither one of them had dependable transportation. Michael barely kept his 1968 Ford legal by patching up holes in the exhaust, and her car was not much better, though it was better looking, to be sure. Another detail to discuss. She got to her car and sped off to his place as fast as a 1970's Chevy could, the money sitting like a stranger in the passenger seat.

Chapter Five

Jezabel was little. Her mother had taken her to the park for a picnic and spread a green blanket on the grass, a cottony blanket with little holes, not the kind you would want to bring to the beach, but a perfect picnic blanket.

One item after another made its way magically out of the cooler, Jezabel's mother passing her first the peanut butter sandwiches, then the bottles of lemonade, then the individual bags of popcorn, then the apples. Jezabel laid them neatly into two place settings, folded the napkins to the side of each grouping, and placed the drinks at the top, just like a real table, just like her mother had taught her. She put the green apples together in the middle, a granny-smith centerpiece, a little celebration of her time with her mom. This was a rare treat.

Her mom sat cross-legged next to her, opening the sandwich bags ceremoniously, handing Jezabel's hers. ""Don't drop crumbs on the blanket, and don't let the lemonade leak," she instructed her daughter who was sure to keep a napkin wrapped around the bottom of the bread. Jezabel did not want to ruin this moment.

"God is great, God is good, let us thank Him for our food, Amen," Jezabel recited.

Grape jelly seeped through the crust and stained the napkin sticky purple. The bread tasted fresh, the peanut butter not like the same stuff she got in her school lunches. It smelled different, something akin to the field and air and earth, and it was a good smell. She guessed it probably was the same peanut butter mom always used, but it tasted better outside with her mother next to her.

After lunch, Jezabel's mother laid back, eyes up at the clouds. Mom said, "What do you think those clouds look like, Jezabel?" Jezabel studied the white puffs carefully in that thinking way she had even as a child.

"A rabbit. That one looks like a rabbit," she said, pointing over her head. "And that one," she said moving her finger, "that one is a horse."

"I think it looks like an angel," her mother said. "See wings?

The halo?"

"Yeah," Jezabel said. "It must be an angel."

She couldn't remember how long they stayed, but she remembered packing up and leaving and wishing whatever that time period was, it had been longer.

Michael wasn't home. She didn't own a cell phone, and neither did he. Neither of them had the money. Actually, Michael had a cell up until last year when he dropped it off a ladder at one of his jobs. He never bothered to replace it.

Jezabel slipped the four $50 bills under his door, wishing she had an envelope and pen. She would call him later to make sure he got it, if she could stay awake, which she doubted she could.

She was right.

Her sleep was instant but strange.

She dreamt of Tony. He was kissing her, but when she looked up, it was Charles who pulled away and grinned.

"Jezzy girl," he said. "I got something for you."

He handed her something soft.

When she looked down, it was her stuffed kitty.

Yolanda prattled on from her chair. Jezabel typed, nodding once in awhile so as not to be rude, but really tuning her out as best she could. Once in awhile, Jezabel would interrupt Yolanda's monologue to ask a question. She wondered if she would be able to get this woman to shut up long enough to recite the disclaimer to her.

"And let me tell you, when that happened, I said, okay. That is the end, mister. No more Mrs. Nice Guy."

How could you have a Mrs. Nice Guy, Jezabel wondered.

"He had been in there for more than fifteen minutes, stinking up the place. I could smell something, but I couldn't tell just what. So here I am, waiting outside the door, arms crossed, tapping my foot, and he finally comes out. He finally comes out, and do you know what he smells like? Can you guess?" Yolanda paused. She stared at Jezabel. "Well, can you?" she demanded.

Oh. Jezabel didn't know she was supposed to actually answer the question. And considering where Yolanda's ex was at the time the smell occurred, Jezabel wasn't sure she wanted to know, either.

"Um, I'm not sure," she said. "What did he smell like?"

"Weed! Pot! Mary Jane. You know? Can you believe it? That whole time he's in the can supposedly taking a crap, he's in there getting stoned. He comes out and his eyes are red..."

Yolanda gestured to her own eyes, somewhat hidden by thin, wire glasses. Her long, straight brown hair, no makeup, gray, fleece top and tattered wide-leg bottoms gave her the look of a modern hippie, someone who might not have a problem with a little weed.

"Yup, that's right. High as a kite. Looking at me with this stupid grin on his face. So let me tell you, I let him have it. 'It's been three weeks since you've worked and you're in the john getting high? What the hell are you thinking?' I screamed at him. And you know what he said? You know what he said?" Yolanda demanded again.

"What?" asked Jezabel, still typing.

"He asked for cookies! Then he just started laughing like an idiot. Laughing! Here we are, the bills piling up and practically no food on the table, the car out of gas and this fool is asking for cookies and laughing. I got so mad, I mean, I was just so mad. I couldn't help it. You know what I did?"

"What?" asked Jezabel again, still typing and not even bothering to look up.

"I slapped him."

"You what?" Jezabel looked up now and chuckled.

"Yup," said Yolanda, dead serious expression on her face. "I slapped him right across the face. And you know what he did? You want to know what he did?"

"What?" asked Jezabel, kind of curious now.

"He laughed! That no-good bastard laughed. And I slapped him hard, too! I can't even believe it."

"Wow," said Jezabel, returning to her keyboard.

She had done it again, gotten suckered into one of these conversations she didn't want to be involved in. Jezabel knew better than to get too wrapped up in it and wanted to slap herself whenever she did, and lately, she felt like she did it a lot. Once a client had your ear, it could be dangerous. They would expect favors from you, sympathy, special treatment, things Jezabel couldn't give any of them if she wanted to keep her job. She treated each one the same, as much as she could, doing her job accurately and she hoped professionally. Or at least as professionally as one could perform her duties in this line of work. This is what she told herself to keep the typing going. She knew on some level she was kidding herself.

It's not that she was cold hearted. She was no simpering Sharon, reciting the disclaimer like she was a partner in the business. She wanted to throw up when she listened to Sharon say the disclaimer. "Now, we need to go over some of the finer points of the contract," Sharon would say. "First, let me tell you a little about our business."

"Our" business. As if she, Sharon, had some stake in it other than a crappy desk, an office, and a line of desperate clients waiting to beg, borrow or steal to meet their basic needs. As if the business were something worth claiming. Then again, maybe Sharon did have some other stake in the business that Jezabel wasn't aware of. Maybe Sharon really was sleeping with Bobby or John or both. Yuck, thought Jezabel. Anyone sleeping with Sharon would have to be blind. Which Bobby and John certainly were not, if their choices in women and cars were any indication.

It wasn't so much that Sharon was ugly. It was the expression on her face, that face that never could smile sincerely, so much so that the wrinkles around her eyes and mouth made her look much more than her forty-something years. She kept her hair short and the gray hair dyed. Her fingernails were always short and rounded, like she went home and filed them daily. Between all that and her clothes, which seemed to be more like uniforms, it was the absolute hypocrisy and sameness about Sharon that made her despicable to Jezabel, that same sameness of this place, of this job, of the clients' lives, those clients who needed people like Sharon. And all of a sudden, Jezabel understood something more about herself.

She was afraid of some day becoming Sharon. She was afraid of doing the same thing, day in and day out, over and over, smiling as insincerely as Sharon did, wrinkles creeping up alongside her eyes, hair graying faster than an Easter egg could be dyed. Jezabel was afraid that in another eighteen or twenty years, after almost two decades of clients and disclaimers, she, Jezabel, would start wearing the same thing every day, using a similar tone every day, doing more of the same thing every day and going home to nothing but a closet full of navy and gray. Nothing to look forward to but another day in the wide, wonderful world of predatory finance.

Jezabel found herself staring at Yolanda. "And so, we've been together now for more than six months, and let me tell you, that man is hot. I mean, he is the real thing, and I am just nuts about him, and I know he works but let me tell you...no man is ever moving in with me again. Never! I will not take that chance, and I will not take that responsibility. It is just not worth it. No one needs that. No one. I mean, if I wanted to have to take care of someone, I would have a baby, right? Do you see me having a baby? Of course not.

"That's because I don't want a baby. And I certainly do not want a man who cannot take care of himself to be my baby. You see these women all the time, smart women, taking these ridiculous excuses for men in, taking care of them, taking care of their finances and their personal problems and their laundry, picking up their underwear, throwing out their trash. I mean, where do these men come from? Where? Don't their mothers know what a disservice they do when they don't teach their sons to care for themselves? But then that's what their mothers did. Their mothers took care of them and their fathers, so these guys are used to having a woman servant around. That's all I was to my ex was a servant. I'll be damned if I'm going to be anyone's servant again. You know what I mean?"

Jezabel looked through her.

"Are you listening?" demanded Yolanda.

"Uh, yes," she said, focusing back on Yolanda's face and not at the wall behind Yolanda.

"Sorry, I was thinking about something you reminded me of. We have to…I mean, we need to…I have to get the printouts for you to sign."

Abruptly, Jezabel pushed her chair back and headed out to the lobby.

"Hey Jezzy! What up, girl?" called Charles, breaking through Jezabel's fugue.

Jezabel couldn't answer. Her mind was spinning yet empty at the same time. What had she been thinking? Sharon? What was Yolanda talking about?

She flashed back to the conversation with Michael on the phone. She had been apologizing. She had totally forgotten about the money and making it home on time, so late he obviously had to go out before her delivery. She thought briefly of telling him about her walk in the park, but then thought better of it. He was already mad, and a story like that would just make it sound like she had lost her mind as well as her track of time.

Thinking of the park made her want to go back again. She thought after dealing with Yolanda she deserved to. Anticipating the possibility of the thing, even if it only existed in her mind, the bus ride didn't seem so bad, the thick slickness of the monkey pole pleasantly cool in her hand, the driver's bellow more than welcome. "Felonias Park, next stop."

The thought got her through the day, through the succession of Yolandas and people whose last dime jingled against useless pennies in their pockets, elderly people wearing their best, threadbare suits, younger women with too much makeup and wearing miniskirts, even younger people who obviously spent their evenings freezing on corners, men who smelled like urine, men who wore too much aftershave, toddlers following their distracted mothers into the office, climbing on extra chairs.

She thought the end of the day never would come, but it had.

As she got off the bus, the cutting wind snuck into her ears and nose. But she didn't have time to worry about head colds. She didn't stop to tie a scarf around her throat or hold her gloved hands over her ears.

She just about ran back to the spot in the park and then stopped. She ignored her aching feet. Her breathing was shallower than a diver preserving tanked oxygen, only whispers of steam coming through her mouth. She held her breath when the branches softly clacked together.

And then, more quickly than before, it stepped through, one, two, three steps, legs, body.

And magically, a magnificent head.

It looked right at her with lashed eyes, like the kind on cows and horses, but the lashes darker and thicker and longer.

Jezabel rubbed her own eyes.

She must have strained them being on the computer all day.

It took another step forward.

It stared at her, no fear, no apology.

The eyes seemed to strip her down to the soul, but it wasn't uncomfortable. She felt strangely warm.

The nose was a kind of triangle with huge whiskers.

And the ears. This was the part she really couldn't believe. They were long and floppy, hanging right down to the middle of the beast's body which was a thickly-knotted, furry thing, tall, certainly not a horse, more like a moose. But the head…there was no mistaking it.

The head looked like that of a lop-eared bunny.

There's no way, she thought. I'm overwrought. I've been under a lot of pressure. This is it. I've finally reached my breaking point, and I've cracked up. Well, I knew it was coming. It was bound to happen with all the stress at work and Sharon and Michael and Charles and every damned day those clients. Oh my, those pathetic clients. It was…

The thing stepped closer to her. She was too encased in warmth and wonder to step back.

Its face was a mottled brown, soft looking, the nose twitching. It stomped it hoofs briefly on the frozen ground and tilted its head at the sight of her.

The rambling in her head shut off, and she just looked. She stared the thing in the eye, now, and it looked back at her, as if it knew something, knew something about her in particular. She found herself cocking her head in imitation of the thing, two creatures, alive, sharing a similar stance, nothing really happening except that Jezabel had the inarticulate feeling that everything was happening and it was happening all at once and it was going to keep happening, that this was not a one-time vision of strangeness that had suddenly come upon her in the woods in March. This was…something.

Well of course it was something, she finally snapped at herself in her mind, words coming back into her head, making more concrete thoughts come back to life. What was this thing? It wasn't anything she had ever seen, and for all she knew, it wasn't anything the world had ever seen. What was it? Combination rabbit and moose? A bunnymoose?

Oh wonderful, she thought. Here, let's look that up on the Internet. "Bunnymoose…a rare species of woodland animal found only in Felonias Park and visible only to women who have officially slipped over the edge. The bunnymoose has been known to be rabid and kill anyone it bites."

Stupid. Even if she had slipped to the other end of sanity, this thing wasn't rabid. No drool. No foaming at the mouth. Everyone knew that animals with rabies foamed at the mouth, and this thing had decidedly no foam.

Well, what are you, she whispered?

The creature turned its head back, glancing over its tail and then looked again at Jezabel.

The uncanny thing was the way it gazed into her eyes, not like an animal at all. Most animals, excluding her cat, avoided looking humans in the eye, something about that being a sign of aggression. This thing looked right at her. No, it was looking through her.

And then, without warning, it abruptly turned, parted the branches once more and slowly walked away.

Her mouth hung open.

She rubbed her eyes again.

"Wait!" she wanted to call to it. But her inhibitions taped her mouth.

She did take a step into the woods, considering going out to the rock. She wanted to look for prints and reassure herself that she had not imagined this thing. But she was afraid. What if she got out there and there weren't any prints? What then? Would that mean she really was nuts? Or would it mean she'd had some kind of spiritual visitation? Oh yeah, she mocked herself. That must be it. Spiritual visitation from a bunnymoose, half bunny, half moose. Oh, holy one, I have come a long way to speak with you about this wonderful creature who chose to visit me in the wilderness. What is it, you ask? It is the bunnymoose, of course. Yeah. That would go over well with a guru.

Silence. She was suddenly aware of being cold, and she huddled into her coat. She looked at her watch, wondering how long she had been here. What? Over an hour? It felt like she had just gotten off the bus.

She pushed herself to turn around and head back in the direction of the walkway. She kept looking over her shoulder. Maybe it would come back. Maybe it would follow her. She told herself to stop it. She didn't need any bunnymoose following her. What would the neighbors think?

Not that she had ever considered what the neighbors might think. Did she even know any of her neighbors? She probably was one of the tenants who had lived there longest. Her next door neighbors had changed at least three times. The people across the hall from her were never home. On the other side of her lived a young mother who seemed to take her kids out early in the morning and not return until late evening, so Jezabel had seen her only once or twice to say hello. No, she didn't really know her neighbors, so a bunnymoose might actually make it into the apartment building unnoticed.

But seriously, there was this thing, this…apparition. Who could she tell? Charles? Michael? Tonya? What could she possibly say? Maybe she shouldn't say anything. Maybe she should just pretend she had come home, made something to eat, cleaned the cat pan, checked email, everything as usual. She was good at keeping her mouth shut. After all, she had to do it all the time in her personal and her professional life.

By the time Jezabel came through the door, she had managed to put the creature out of her mind or at least on the back shelf. It was time to focus on the here and now, and the blinking on her answering machine told her what that might be.

She dropped her coat on the couch, went to the phone and pressed "play."

"Hey! Where are ya? Give me a call or just come over." Beep. Click.

It was getting late, it was dark, and she had no gas, so she had to stop for gas first. On her way to Michael's house, she took a detour back through her neighborhood and drove by the park. She peered through her window, squinting beyond the arched entrance of Felonias Park. What had she been expecting to see there? The reincarnation of a beautiful day?

Michael lived in a pea green, run-down Victorian that had been turned into apartments. It could have been a nice place, but the landlord had lost all interest in it years ago. Now the six apartments there housed single men. Three of the men, Jezabel was sure, were drug dealers. One was a friendly guy Jezabel was sure was gay, but she almost never saw him. The other was an elderly man who had lived there for ten years, supplementing his rent payment with state benefits. Jezabel sometimes wondered if the old man had family in the area, if anyone ever checked on him, if anyone would even know if he died. She asked Michael this once. He shrugged and said it wasn't any of his business. Jezabel was glad the man never came in as a client.

She knocked at the door, and she could hear Michael unlatching it. The latch had that clunky sound that old deadbolts and chain-locks have against thick, brittle doors. It was a strangely familiar sound to her.

Michael opened up. He wasn't smiling. She wondered if they were in for a fight.

"I got the money. Little late, huh?"

"Um, yeah. Hello to you, too," she said, somewhat irritated.

He got the message. "Oh, hi," he kissed her on the cheek. "Thanks for coming over with it, even if it was late."

"No problem," she said.

She wondered why she lied like this, but she kind of felt like he had acknowledged her irritation and made up for it with the kiss, so she didn't want to make it any worse. No sense inciting trouble if there was a way to avoid it.

"You want something to drink?" he asked. She nodded. She hadn't had anything since lunch. She sat on his metal kitchen chair. The set looked like something from a 1950's diner, beat-up vinyl on the top, silver surrounding it. The vinyl was orange. So were the chairs in her office and in the lobby at work, she thought. What the heck was it with orange, anyway? Popular color for poverty or what?

"So I'll be at your place tomorrow night," he said, pouring some soda into a smudged glass. She nodded.

"You're quiet," he said.

"Tired."

"You want to crash here tonight?" he asked. "Just for old time's sake?"

She was impressed. He almost never asked her that anymore. Maybe he thought it would relax her about the move. She didn't know. She just knew she was tired. "I'd have to leave early enough to go home to get clothes," she said. "I don't have any in my car."

"I think you left a few things in the laundry basket," he said. "Want me to look?"

"Sure," she said, taking off her coat and hanging it over the chair back. She took a sip of the soda and waited for him.

"It's wrinkled, but you can throw it in the laundry and it'll be good," he said. "Or you could just put it between the mattresses to press it and it'll be fine."

She smiled. "Ah, I think I'll take it down to the laundry." She was quite sure it was not a clean outfit, though she was also quite sure he would have worn it if he were her.

"Cool. Let me give you some more stuff to throw in with yours. No sense wasting the load."

The laundry room in Michael's house was a scary place. While hers was right down the well-lit, albeit worn, hallway, his was in a dirt basement. To get there, she had to pass the other apartments, go down the narrow, creaky, wooden steps, pull the string on the light bulb and walk farther down into the dank, cold air that surrounded a reconditioned washer and dryer set more than a decade old. The set was avocado colored, and the light was so dim in the basement, if you didn't know where to look to find the appliances, you might walk right past them.

The good part was that, unlike her own laundry room, this one was always empty. Jezabel doubted any of the tenants ever used it. She sometimes wondered if Michael even used it. Whenever she was over, he always had laundry to do, and he inevitably brought some to her place on weekends.

The next day, in her now-clean but still slightly wrinkled outfit, Jezabel suddenly remembered laundry, and the conversation and her loan to Michael brought Jezabel back to the present and the lobby and the copier.

Another one just as chatty and irate as Yolanda, but this one was someone whose name she made sure she forgot. The girl came in wearing a t-shirt that went only down to her bellybutton in spite of the season. She had a crystal belly button ring, and in spite of the tiny baby in the car seat, no stretch marks or fat. She couldn't have been older than fifteen.

Jezabel was sure the girl was using a fake ID. Tonya was good, but she couldn't always judge ages and figured if the client was decent looking and had a way to pay, she wasn't about to do background checks, especially on single moms. Tonya had spent too many years as a single mom herself.

Jezabel thought she better make her copies and get the girl signed and out the door. Couldn't take another Yolanda or the thought of this girl being a mother.

"Okay, here we go," Jezabel said, re-entering her office. "I have your copies and my copies to sign."

"Good! Great! This will really help," she said unnaturally quickly. Was she nervous or on drugs? Jezabel couldn't tell."

"I can get rid of all those old utility bills stupid-face ran up and just pay this off and be done with it."

Jezabel wondered why the girl hadn't tried the budget plan from the electric company, but maybe she didn't know any better. Then again, Jezabel had tried the plan and didn't think it ended up helping her any. It just made her more broke throughout the year, so now, she suffered the winters the best she could.

Jezabel didn't qualify for heating assistance—she made too much money at her job, pathetic as it was. She was sure this young mother would qualify, though, considering she was living on subsidy and had a baby. But maybe the emergency services provider figured out she was using a fake ID. Those organizations had many more scruples and rules than In-a-Pinch.

Maybe some day I won't have to worry about payment plans, thought Jezabel. Maybe when Michael and I live together, things really will improve, and in a year, we can even think about getting a better place.

Back to the present, she reminded herself. Damn her mind. It always seemed to want to wander somewhere far from In-a-Pinch.

"Now there are some things I need to tell you," Jezabel said, interrupting her own mind and suddenly aware the girl had picked up the baby. She slipped the tiny thing under her shirt, and Jezabel could hear suckling. Couldn't she have waited just another minute, Jezabel thought? How embarrassing.

"Sorry," the girl said, reading Jezabel's expression. "My boobs started hurting."

"I have to remind you that In-a-Pinch is not…" Jezabel stared without acknowledging the girl's comment. She averted her eyes.

"You know how high he used to keep the heat? In a tiny place like ours and even with an electric blanket, he wanted the heat on 80 all the time. Eighty degrees. So he could walk around in shorts."

"I'm sorry, but I really need to get through this part of the contract," Jezabel said. "I know how it can be, but we need to focus."

God, Jezabel thought. I sound like a freaking school teacher.

"Now, I have to remind you that In-a-Pinch is not a bank. You are taking out a high interest loan…"

"Well it can't be any worse than his damn habits," nursing-girl interjected.

Jezabel continued, wondering for a second what those habits might be, but she suspected she already knew.

"...to be repaid over a six-month period. You will be responsible for the principal of the loan, monthly interest accrued at 27% and the initiation fee of $75."

"He had a loan at 30%. Can you believe it? I mean, who would take out a loan like that? If I was with him when they offered him that loan, I would have..."

Then why was she here, Jezabel wondered. Never mind. None of her business. Some women couldn't add.

"Ma'am, please! Let's get through this," Jezabel said more loudly this time.

"If you miss one or more payments, we reserve the right to aggressively collect from you and/or the cosigners designated on your application form," she finished quickly.

Whew! She made it. "Do you have any questions?"

"Where do I sign?"

"Right here," Jezabel said, and breathed a sigh of relief. For the first time since she had entered the door, the girl was silent, and so was Jezabel's mind.

This wasn't the first time he had said it. She looked at him through sleepy eyes. He was next to her, naked, as she was. The half smile that said he was satisfied for the moment played on his face, around his mustache through his beard. She touched his beard, feeling the skin beneath the coarse hair, and started scratching him lightly. Though she didn't like the beard covering his face, she liked the way it felt under her fingers, piercing the thin skin beneath her nails.

"Don't do that," he said, snapping her hand with his, holding her still. "Don't treat me like the damn cat."

"Let go," she laughed softly. "I know you aren't a cat."

"You need to get rid of that cat," he said. "Cats are just creepy, and that cat of yours is a real bitch."

"Michael!" she protested. "Tarika isn't just a cat to me. We've been through a lot together."

"So have we," said Michael, flipping over onto his stomach and turning his face from hers. "Don't I mean as much to you as that cat?"

"Well, Tarika doesn't ask me to get rid of you!" Jezabel teased, trying to coax him back into his peaceful mood.

"She might as well, the bitch," he said. "You see how she hates me."

"That's because you don't like her!" Jezabel protested. "Come on, Michael, she's a cat for goodness sakes. She can't be in...in competition with you!"

"Sure she can," Michael said, but it was hard to tell if he was kidding. He muffled his face into the mattress. "Besides, you can't have a cat if you are going to have a baby."

Jezabel paused. "But, I'm not having a baby," she said.

"Well, not right now you aren't," he said. "But you will some day, and when you get pregnant, you won't be able to have a cat around. You know how that goes. No cleaning cat litter. It's the cat shit that's dangerous. Even I know that."

"Well, you could always clean the litter pan," she suggested.

"Ha! Yeah, right. I don't think so."

"Do you hate all cats?" she asked him.

"Hate animals in general," he responded. "Animals aren't supposed to be in your house. They belong in the freezer or in your belly. That's what they were put here for."

Jezabel suddenly remembered the picture she had seen of her father, Jarrod McPhearson, a picture in which he wore hunting clothes and was holding a dead, gray duck.

"My father used to hunt," she said quietly.

"Yeah? Sounds like a good guy. You ever find out anything about him?"

"No," Jezabel said, sad voiced. "I tried to look up his name once, but there were too many. I asked my mom for his social security number so I could buy one of those searches, you know, the ones they advertise where they can find anyone?"

"Yeah, I know those," he said. "What did she say?"

Jezabel paused again. Michael didn't often ask about her family or her past or anything that had taken place before their meeting. It was like that part of her life didn't exist for him.

She rolled over on to her stomach and pressed her chin into the backs of her hands resting on the pillow, remembering what her mother had said to her.

"She told me to stop chasing ghosts."

"What the hell does that mean?" he asked.

She sighed. "I don't know. You know my mom."

He grunted.

As a matter of fact, Michael didn't know her mom at all. He had met her once, and she had been so silent that he really never got more than an answer to "How are you?" from her. She could only imagine what her mother would say when Jezabel broke the news about Michael moving in.

"Yeah, well, if she likes me as much as she liked your dad, then I guess you can understand some things about her," Michael said. "You know what? Forget about them, both of them. Fuck 'em and their stupidity. You don't need them anyways."

"Sometimes, though, I wish..."

"You don't need 'em," he said, rolling over to face her. He kissed her cheek. "You got me. And you definitely don't need some stupid cat."

She wanted to laugh and tell him to stop joking, but she knew he wasn't joking. So she put her head on the pillow and closed her eyes, wishing herself to sleep.

"So what? You mad at me or something?" Charles said, hanging on her doorframe.

"Huh?" asked Jezabel, looking up.

"I try talking to you, and you just walk off like old Charles is invisible or something," he complained.

"Oh! I'm sorry, Charles. I guess I am just distracted is all."

"Oh I see, yeah, I understand. Lots on your mind now that you and the old man decided to shack up, huh?"

She nodded. Then she said, "I mean, no. No, it's not that."

What was wrong with her? Talking to Charles about anything other than Sharon was a no-no. The last thing she needed was him to know any more about her than he already did, and... She caught herself. Her inner monologue was starting to sound like Yolanda or the teen mother. What the hell?

"Don't worry, I won't tell anyone," Charles said.

"Charles," sighed Jezabel, "there's nothing to tell. Okay? I had a really chatty client in here a couple of days ago. And I mean really chatty. I couldn't hear myself think. And you know how little thinking you need to do on this job. Then I had another one shortly after. I think I'm a bit overwhelmed."

Charles smiled. "Yeah, I know. I just ignore people like them. So how about you give yourself a break and come out to lunch with me?"

Jezabel paused. She and Charles had gone to lunch before. It wasn't a big deal. And she was really needing to get out of the office. She had her doubts about him and his intentions, but she figured since they had lunched before and she was so permanently and obviously attached at this point, it really didn't make any difference. And she could use a change of scenery for sure.

"Okay. Let's go," she said.

"Okay," said Charles, grinning. "Okay. Now there's my old Jezzy. Let me get my coat. Still damn cold out there."

Jezabel put on her coat and walked out to the lobby. Tonya was at her desk, steadfast as ever. How could Sharon even insinuate Tonya was anything but reliable? The woman was always there on time dealing with the brunt of the clients, holding them at bay when the office was short staffed, keeping them occupied when Jezabel or Charles went out to lunch, hardly ever going out to lunch herself... and rarely was she ever snide. What more could Sharon expect?

It occurred to her that Sharon might be jealous of the respect Bobby and John gave Tonya. Sharon didn't like to share. Sharon didn't like to be nice. She faked it, which made her haughtier than the queen in Alice in Wonderland. Sharon treated most people like lint between sweaty toes.

"Tonya, Charles and I are getting out of here for lunch," she said. "What can we get you?"

"Uh oh!" Tonya said. "You and Charles. Michael know about this?" Tonya teased.

A teasing from Tonya was not like a teasing from Sharon. Tonya's teasing might be more than a tease, but she was never sarcastic or condescending. Sharon's teasing always had a nasty, double edge.

"Yeah, you know how we are, slackers of the place," Charles piped in. "Never do anything round here except yap and lunch, yap and lunch. Just like you, Tonya, my girl. Ain't never see you do anything round here either. Better watch out or you will get reported by the," he gestured ironically towards Sharon's office, "the really big boss here."

"Just you rest your neck," Tonya said. "And get me a steak and cheese over that Subway over there. I'm so hungry, I'm ready to start munching staples."

"Not a problem. We'll hook you up," Charles said.

Sitting in the Subway waiting for their sandwiches, Charles and Jezabel both looked around at the customers. "Is it me," Charles said in a tone lower than his comic stage whisper, "or is this crowd starting to look a little more mangy?"

"Oh no, it's looking more mangy," Jezabel agreed.

It was true. The poverty of the place seemed to be spreading, and Jezabel wasn't sure if it was coming from their office and spilling into the streets of the city or the other way around. For sure, though, there were some poor looking folks in here today.

One man slouched in the back booth, apparently nursing a coffee, nothing else at his table. His beat-up backpack lay in the aisle next to him, his tattered army jacket, stained with coffee, and God knew what else, crumpled behind his back. The man wore sunglasses even though the sun was not bright and he was inside. He linked his weathered hands loosely around his cup, and Jezabel thought he might be sleeping. It was, after all, a heck of a lot warmer in here than it was outside, and if the man hadn't slept in a bed in awhile, a booth in a sub shop would be a luxury.

Guys like that couldn't even get a loan at In-a-Pinch, Jezabel thought. You had to have some kind of income or situation to show you could pay the loan, even if was just a good, believable lie. And you had to have an address. They didn't give loans to obviously homeless people. Even Bobby and John couldn't legally justify that.

It occurred to her, though, that some of her clients who defaulted could easily become homeless as a result or might be lying about their address. Some of them gave just a P.O. box number, and it was pretty cheap to maintain those. She threw the thought out of her mind. This was not time to add weight to her already heavy brain.

"Jezabel, you with me?" Charles asked, snapping his fingers in front of her face.

"Yeah, I'm here," she said.

She looked at him.

"Charles, you ever think about our business?" she asked.

"Oh yeah, I think all the time, and next time those clowns Bobby and John come in, I'm going to give them some of my own business and tell them what they can do with their crappy-assed offices and that witch they call an employee..."

"No, no, that's not what I mean," Jezabel said.

The girl behind the counter called their number. Their subs were ready. They both got up to collect their food and get a drink at the soda fountain.

Back at the table, Jezabel decided to drop the subject. This obviously was one more thing not to talk to Charles about.

"So what are you thinking?" he asked when he got back. He squeaked a straw through the plastic hole in the drink cup cover.

"Huh?"

"About the business," he said. "You know. What have you thought about it?"

"Oh," she said, surprised he remembered her train of thought. "Well I just wonder about the people that come in. How they can pay the loan. What it does to them financially. If it's the right thing to do, giving these people loans like this."

"What made you think about that?" he asked.

She shrugged. "Don't know. Guess I have to think about something while I'm entering the same information every day, saying the same things every day. Besides, some of those people make you think, don't they?" she asked.

"Only if you listen to them," he said. "See that's the difference between me and you. You're too quiet. That gives them the chance to talk. Me, I do all the talking. Hell, I never shut up," he laughed, stomping his foot in appreciation of his own character.

She smiled.

"You need to do more of that. Just sit there and talk and talk. Don't let them say anything."

"But how do you get the information you need then? I mean, we have to ask them questions," she said.

"Oh that?" he laughed again, taking a quick bite of his sub and chewing. "They give me the answer, then I butt back in and start talking again. Never let them say more than just the answer, is all. It's that simple."

He chewed some more, taking a sip of his drink. His long lashes looked even longer when he lowered his eyes to drink from the straw. Jezabel wondered, in passing, what he looked like when he was sleeping. Probably like an angel, she thought. How ironic!

"But what do you talk about?" she said. "I wouldn't even know what to say, and to be honest, I don't know if I could type and talk at the same time like that."

"You ever listen to what I say?" he asked.

"Not really," she admitted.

"Well, you ain't missing much. The biggest bunch of horseshit is what I say all day long. Whatever comes to mind comes spilling out this here mouth, and half the time it doesn't even make sense to me," he grinned.

"Sometimes I listen to myself and I say, 'Charles, you really are spouting off a lot of nonsense today' and then I answer myself, 'That's right. Gotta keep on talking because if I don't, he will, and I don't want to hear anything he might say.' I go all day like this, babbling to the clients then asking myself what the hell I'm saying and you know what I come up with?" he asked.

"What?" she asked.

"Nothing. Just a whole lot of absolutely nothing."

She giggled. That was Charles, all right. Simple, basic, funny, never giving enough thought to something to let it bother him. She wished she could be more like that, stop mulling things over. And now here she was mulling things over about how she mulled things over! How stupid was that?

She took a bite of her sandwich again and looked at the man in the back booth.

He was slumped back in the seat a little more now, his mouth open and slack, asleep. Or dead.

What if he was dead? Would anyone know? She looked at the girl behind the counter. Would the girl come over eventually and tell him he had to leave, only to find the guy was stiff as the booth table? She pictured the girl, screaming and running for the phone. But realistically, the worst part was that the girl probably wouldn't even go over there to throw the guy out. She probably didn't even notice him there back in the booth and wouldn't ever notice. Her shift would end, someone else would come in, and that someone else would glance at the man and just leave him alone. They wouldn't know if something happened until the place was ready to close. Then someone would have to say, "Sir, we're closing now. Sir," shaking him by the shoulder. When he didn't move, then they would know, and not until then.

Scary. Jezabel had the urge to go over and shake his shoulder now, to see if he was okay. But that was stupid. He was most likely just sleeping and would be pissed if she woke him up. Probably punch her in the face. Better leave him be.

She glanced to her right. Two young mothers (but not as young as her recent client) sat in a booth with pre-school boys. The boys were dressed in new, bright clothes, reds and electric blues. The mothers were dressed in beat up jeans and dingy coats. One of the mothers had long, black, wavy hair that looked like it hadn't been combed in days. The tangles made a nest at the base of her neck. Jezabel wondered if it would be better for her to just cut it off and start over than to try to manage that knot. The other mother had long, straight, blond hair, about the color of Jezabel's. But this lady's hair looked greasy, and the lady had bags under her eyes, more prominent because of her pale skin. At least the kids look good, Jezabel thought. The moms looked in rough shape.

"So you gonna try it my way, or what?" Charles interrupted her silent monologue.

Jezabel turned her attention back to him. "Yeah, I'll give it a try. I'm sure I won't be as successful as a professional motor mouth like you, but I can learn."

"Good. When I'm free, I'll come in and coach you," he said.

"Oh...no!" she said, horrified. That's all she needed. Charles hanging around, listening to her stumble through a litany of nothing and then the disclaimer. Sharon coming in and clearing her throat like some crotchety librarian. Talk about a recipe for a bad afternoon.

Tonya was grateful for the sub when they returned. Jezabel asked her if she wanted her to cover the front desk, but she said Sharon had already volunteered, and she didn't want to disappoint poor Sharon. Tonya grinned. "And don't worry. I'll be sure to clean off my desk first." Jezabel laughed. Everyone knew what Sharon was all about. She would not hesitate to go through Tonya's or anyone else's stuff.

The afternoon couldn't go quickly enough. She wanted the weekend to come. She wanted Michael to come over and to watch television with him and snuggle and talk about their plans and...

The phone rang. "This is Jezabel," she said.

"Hey! Listen, I'm going to be later tonight than I thought. Got some things to wrap up before I come over and then go to that job next week."

"Oh," she said. "Okay, well what time do you think?"

"Not sure, but it'll be tonight," he said.

"Okay. I'll keep a plate for you in the fridge."

"Okay. See you later," he said and hung up. She frowned. She had been looking forward to this and now he was going to be late again. But then, last night had been nice.

After the dishes, they had gone to bed and he crawled in beside her, naked. He peeled her clothes off in that way that always gave her chills, and they had both slept soundly after. It was only during the day, after listening to everyone's stories...

Besides, this would give her more time to get home, relax, cook something nice, pet the cat.

She had an idea. She would get off the earlier stop and go to the park again. That would be a nice treat. Felonias Park on a Friday afternoon. It was still cold, but if she bundled up...

And maybe she would see it again.

She scolded herself. Jezabel, that thing was not real. It was a figment of your weird imagination so just stop it now. Knock it off. Enjoy the park and go home and cook for your honey.

She decided she would do just that.

But she couldn't stick to her previous decision. The park — the thing — called to her tired mind.

Chapter Six

The man standing by the cast iron arch had his head down, back to the wind. His backpack seemed to take the brunt of the cold, and his hands were stuffed deep in his pockets. He glanced up as Jezabel approached. She stared. It was him. The man from the sub shop. He wasn't dead. Whew.

He looked back down and started walking away from the arch, away from Jezabel, heading up the street. Had he recognized her too? It was impossible to know, given the sunglasses, which he still wore.

She didn't want him to recognize her. She was well aware of safety measures, of not walking the same routes at the same times, avoiding stalkers, etc. It was difficult in some ways because anyone who came into In-a-Pinch would know where she worked. And it would be easy to track her to the bus, since she didn't drive to work. But otherwise…

She had to stop. She was getting paranoid.

She passed under the arch and looked up at the lettering, wondering again about this person Felonias. What kind of people had parks named after them? What kind of people had such odd parks named after them? Maybe someone who had lived in the neighborhood long ago? Someone who once had a good tract of land to donate?

Jezabel knew some parks had little signs that described the park's history, but not this one. This was still some unpopular little place. The only times she had seen it be anywhere near busy was on sunny, warm, summer days. Then she would see college students walking hand in hand, but not many. This wasn't the main park in the city by any means, and it wasn't even the most interesting.

That was one reason Jezabel liked the place so much. It gave her solace. And of course, she liked it because it reminded her of Michael and the picture of them together. And now, she had another reason to like it. Or at least another reason to think about it.

Once again, she told herself to stop it. If she was here just to see that creature, whatever it was, she would be sadly disappointed. And she didn't want to waste her visit here with any amount of disappointment and certainly not with hallucinations. The other day, she had loved the place simply because of the layout, the feel and the memory. She wanted the same thing now. She didn't want the anticipation of wondering and the excitement of...whatever.

Maybe she shouldn't even take that route, she thought. Maybe instead of going right, she should take the walkway on the left instead, see if there were any sections of that walk she had left unexplored. Then she wouldn't be able to walk past the woods and look and wonder.

Oh, who was she kidding? Even as she thought this, her feet had carried her faster in the direction of the woods. She told herself it was because it was colder this time, that she had to walk fast to keep warm. Her scarf had slipped down from her ears, and her earrings felt like they had frozen to her lobes. At this rate, she wouldn't even make it to the woods. She would just turn right around. And even if she didn't turn around, she would hardly have the heat in her body to make herself stand there and stare into the woods.

But of course, that's what she was doing right now. Staring into the woods. Looking at the rock all the way back, searching for furry legs, hooves, something, anything that resembled the creature she so vividly remembered. She thought of the whiskers, the way the breath of the thing left a velvet patch of moistness against its nose and the whisker tips. It had looked warm enough, and the fur on the back, longer and shaggier, looked soft. She would love to touch it and to feel that warmth it seemed to have leant her that last time.

She stood for awhile. Her feet started to numb, and she stomped them on the walkway. She imagined the beast, whatever it was, the bunnymoose, doing the same thing, stomping in the cold, leaving impressions in the dirt like fossils. If she saw the impressions, wouldn't she prove to herself that the thing was real? Maybe she would walk into the woods and up to the rock again, look. Maybe at least the prints were there.

She didn't want to be premature about this. After all, how long had it taken for the bunnymoose to appear before? Ten minutes? Fifteen? She really couldn't remember. Time just seemed to drain away that other day, but now, it trickled.

This was exactly what she had wanted to avoid, the waiting and feeling disappointed.

She wondered why she even felt disappointed. Shouldn't she feel relieved, instead, because the thing really was just an illusion? Did she actually want to see some kind of odd creature that didn't exist or that she would at least have a hard time proving existed?

But then, she didn't have to tell anyone, so she guessed she didn't have a problem. The bunnymoose was her secret. She liked that, having a creature as a secret, even if it were odd, possibly not even real.

It occurred to her she was far too old to be having this kind of fantasy, the type that encouraged most people to visit a mental health specialist. This is what crazy people do, she thought. This is how it starts. You think about something so much that you start to see it, and before you know it, the thing becomes real to you. You can't separate reality from fantasy. Isn't that what insanity is? Am I going insane?

She glanced at her watch. She had been standing there for twenty minutes. It would be colder soon, and darker, and the last thing she needed to do was to walk home in the dark. Besides, she had to cook for Michael and get cleaned up even if he was coming in late. She felt messy somehow, disheveled. Probably been looking at too many rundown people today, she thought.

She had to at least walk as far as the rock.

So she did, one tentative step after another, the still-frozen layer of snow crunching under her feet.

A twig snapped and she jumped.

She thought she heard a rustle only to discover it was a tiny bird walking, not flying, through the low branches of some nearby bush. Damn, she thought. Even if it was here, it wouldn't necessarily come out.

Maybe it was really private, she thought. Yeah, she laughed at herself. So private, no one but she had ever seen it. Wacko.

The stone came upon her soon enough, and she looked down at its base. Nothing. Of course not, she thought. And that's because you imagined the whole thing. Now go home and get your brain and your kitchen together. She turned resolutely.

Something snapped behind her. She whirled around.

Squirrel.

No bunny. No moose. Just a squirrel juxtaposed with a weird young lady, one with an over-active imagination.

She sighed and made her way back to the walk.

She walked slowly, lowering her head against the wind, plodding along, her mind emptied by disappointment, almost depression. She passed the walkway, the bench, the arch, scuffing her feet in her old pumps, making her way down the neighborhood street, barely noticing the Victorians she usually looked at along the way. In the past, she would have imagined buying one of those houses and cleaning it up, painting it and bringing back its youth. But not now.

She threw her keys onto the table, her coat on the chair and flopped onto her itchy couch. Tarika greeted her, rubbing against her leg and then unapologetically jumping into her lap. Jezabel absently stroked the cat's head, feeling the purr erupting from the cat's throat and belly, reverberating through her whole body and ending in the tail. Purring was such a strange behavior, Jezabel thought. Still, it would be great to be able to purr, if one had the need or desire.

She had no idea what time it was, but she realized she had fallen asleep and Michael hadn't called and hadn't come by yet. In a way, she was thoroughly relieved. She hadn't done a thing, hadn't cooked, hadn't cleaned up or changed the sheets. Not that he would notice the sheet change, but Jezabel felt it was necessary to do those things before he came over. She didn't want him to think she was a slob, and even though he didn't bother cleaning his place before she came over (she wondered when the last time he changed his own sheets was) that didn't stop her from her rituals.

Throwing open the cabinet, she pulled out a saucepan and a frying pan. Boiled rice, browned chicken and veggies, she thought. Balanced, easy to cook and healthy. Michael preferred burgers, she was sure, but after eating out for lunch this week and living off places like Dunkin Donuts and Subway, she looked forward to a home cooked, wholesome meal. And Michael needed to eat better anyway. He didn't take care of himself the way he should.

She had tried to get him to take vitamins, but after one of those "horse pills" as he called them, he wouldn't try again. So she had bought some children's vitamins for him, which he said tasted terrible. She told him he was much worse than any child and if he got sick, then what would he do? He didn't have health insurance, and she didn't want him sick. He had said to her, "Oh, so if I get sick, you dump me, huh?"

"That's not what I mean, and you know it!" she had said, slapping him lightly on the shoulder.

As far as she knew, he still had a full bottle of children's vitamins in the cabinet at his place.

The chicken was sizzling when she heard his knock at the door. Ten o'clock. She wondered what he had to do that had kept him so long, but it was okay because she apparently had needed to sleep. She unlatched the door and greeted him with a hug. He hugged her briefly and came in.

"So how are you?" she asked.

She looked at his face. He looked tired, too, which didn't make too much sense. He hadn't worked today, had he?

"Okay," he said.

"You look tired," she said.

"Yeah, I am," he said.

"You get everything done you had to?"

"Yeah. Had to get it all done because that job starts Monday and I wouldn't have time. And I knew I was coming over here this weekend."

She nodded. "Made some dinner," she said.

"Thought it would be in the fridge," he said.

"No, I got a late start. I actually fell asleep."

"You slept all this time?" he asked, surprised.

"Well, not all this time," she admitted. Should she tell him?

"Where'd you go?" he asked, narrowing his eyes. She looked at his eyes, trying to read him. She got nothing from looking at the expression around his mouth. Again, the beard, like a barrier from truth, seemed to get in the way lately, and it was harder for her to see his reactions and emotions.

"I got off the bus and walked through the park," she said.

"Oh," he said, looking at the stove.

She breathed out, relieved he wasn't mad. Then she was mad at herself for wondering if he would be mad. Why would he be, and if he was, why would she care since he would have no right to be mad?

"Our park," she said.

"What's for dinner?" he asked.

"Chicken, rice and veggies," she said. "I walked through our park," she repeated.

"Oh."

He plunked down in a kitchen chair and unlaced his boots, slowly weaving the laces apart, pulling the tongue out and removing the boots like they had been weighing him down spiritually. He threw them in the kitchen corner with a loud "thunk." Dried mud cracked off the bottom and spilled on the floor. Jezabel looked at it and turned back to the stove.

"So what's so great at the park?" he asked, not in a particularly curious tone.

"Oh nothing, really," she said. "I just felt like walking there."

"Which one was it?"

She was disappointed he didn't remember. "You know, that little park we walked in and took that picture. The one I have on my computers."

"Huh-uh," he said, shaking his head. "No clue."

"You know, the one we walked in on our first date. It has this big arch made out of black cast iron and the benches…Felonias Park," she said. "You remember now?" He shook his head again. She frowned. "Well you showed me it," she said. She thought since they had their picture taken there and it was so early in their relationship, that it had meant something to him, too. It bothered her that he didn't even remember the place. But maybe he just had other things on his mind. He shrugged and looked around for more napkins.

"So what'd you have to get done?" she asked.

Michael went into the cabinet, got a glass and helped himself to some juice from the refrigerator. "Saw this guy about a motorcycle," he said. "He's selling it real cheap, and I thought it would be cheaper than the truck. Then I had to get the truck over to Sal's to get the heads fixed, and I owed him from the last time, and he didn't want to do any work until I gave him money up front. I told him I'm sick and tired of this damn thing breaking down on me all the time. Told him about the bike, and he says it would be cheaper and maybe even cheaper to fix." Michael took a swig of the juice.

So that explained it, his needing the money and needing it right away. He had to have something to get to work with, and he couldn't get the truck fixed unless he paid up front. It made sense to her now, and she wished he had told her before. She would have spent less time dawdling in the park the other day and more time focusing on what she had to get done.

"A motorcycle?" she asked. "Isn't that dangerous?"

"Only if you drive like an idiot," he said.

"Don't you need a special license for that?"

"Yeah, but I can get it easy. Besides, the thing's good on gas. I can get wherever I need and go from one job to another."

"But you won't be able to haul stuff," she reminded him. "Don't you use the truck to haul stuff when you're on a job?"

"Won't do that anymore," he said. "Shouldn't have to do it anyway. That's the problem with these guys. They hire you to do a job, and before you know it, you're hauling their shit around all over the Goddamned place and they don't pay you any extra for it. So now when they ask if I got a truck for hauling, I just say no."

"But won't that mean you won't get certain jobs?" she asked, worried.

"Nah, shouldn't have any effect on that," he said, confidently. He took another drink. "I never have problems finding work, except in winter," he said. "Weather getting warmer now, I'll be all set."

She walked over to the refrigerator to get the butter. He grabbed her and pulled her onto his lap, started kissing her neck. "Don't you worry about anything," he said. His beard brushing against her skin made her acutely aware he was running his tongue up to her earlobe, and she sat like that with her eyes closed until she thought the chills would actually make her shiver.

"Enough of that, you," she said, giggling, twisting away from him. "I'm going to burn the rice!"

"Let it burn then," he said, holding her still tighter. She turned her face to his and he kissed her in that possessive way he had, his lips on hers like he owned her.

And she thought, for all intensive purposes, he did.

Jezabel grew up on only stories about her father, and they weren't nice stories. She could recite some of the more colorful ones by heart, such as the time her father had to watch her.

She was three. He got a call from one of the guys to go meet him at a bar. He told his pal he had to watch his daughter, that his wife was working. His pal said to bring "the kid."

According to Jezabel's mother, her father brought her to the bar. And while Jezabel had heard lots of stories of irresponsible parents taking their children into bars, this story was a little different. Her father had left her locked in the car.

There had been a big fight after that, none of which Jezabel remembered, but it resulted in her father being told to leave. Several years later, Jezabel's mother said she heard her estranged husband was living on the streets, drinking from a bottle barely hidden in a paper bag.

"That's where he belongs," her mother said.

Jezabel didn't ask about her father that often because about the last thing she wanted to hear was that story again. She would have liked to hear something good about him, that he bought her a toy or painted the bathroom or made good cornbread or something. She couldn't believe he was all that bad. After all, he and her mother had been married. There must have been something between Mr. and Mrs. McPhearson.

Once, when Jezabel was about ten, she asked if her mother had a picture of her father.

"What do you want that for?"

"Just kind of want it," she had mumbled in that way kids have when they are uncomfortable with a discussion.

Her mother had gone into the bedroom and dug into an old shoebox filled with pictures. Most of them were black and white and had people in them Jezabel didn't know. From the bottom, she pulled a wallet size photo, crinkled, the color fading. She handed it to Jezabel silently, put the box back in the drawer and walked out of the room.

Jezabel remembered sitting on her mother's bed for a long

time staring at that picture. A mustached man, wearing hunting clothes, stood grinning, holding a shotgun in one hand and holding up the dead mallard in the other. His face was creased, and it wasn't just the picture. It was the face of a man who spent a lot of time outside and around smoke. Jezabel remembered the bar story. She put it out of her mind and took the picture into her own room, which didn't smell so much like her mother — used pantyhose and room freshener.

Her own bedroom had been painted yellow. As long as she could remember, it had been yellow, and Jezabel felt comforted by the cheery color. Whenever she felt upset, she would go to her room, not necessarily because she wanted the security and amusement of her toys and bed, but because of the yellow walls that seemed to smile at her. She would sit at the edge of her bed and stare at the far wall, the one with the window curtained in pale, yellow, Pricilla sheers. She would just sit and stare like that until the bad feeling went away. She didn't remember crying or pulling covers over her head. Just sitting there. Sometimes, she sat there with her stuffed kitty, sometimes not.

Jezabel kept the picture of her father in a little notebook where she stored other things she felt were secret — notes from boys in her class, notes she had wanted to send a boy but didn't, notes from her girlfriends, and short journal entries describing details like what was on the school lunch menu. The notebook never left the narrow, center drawer of her white enameled desk. If she had owned a lock, she would have used it, but she didn't. She would know if something had been disturbed, though.

One day after school, she went into her room, shut the door and opened the drawer, looking for her notebook. It wasn't there. She just stared at the space in the drawer where the notebook had been, somehow believing that if she stared long enough, it would reappear the way a small thing would materialize if you looked hard enough. There was just no way it was missing.

After several minutes of this, Jezabel accepted the notebook was indeed gone. But just to make sure, she took the drawer out and felt beneath the wooden slats to make sure it hadn't slipped through the drawer. She didn't feel anything other than the frantic catch in her throat. Where was her notebook? Where? She put the drawer back in. Her mother? But why?

She opened her bedroom door and called out, "Mom, have you seen a notebook?"

Her mother came to the top of the stairs. "Such as this one?" her mother asked her, waving it in front of her.

"Yes! Mom, what are you doing with my notebook?"

"Maybe the real question is," her mother said, her voice low like it got when she was about to erupt in anger, "why do you have notes from boys in here? And why are you writing notes to boys when you should be doing your schoolwork?"

"That's not fair. That's my notebook!" Jezabel had screamed. "Give it to me!"

"I will not give it to you. And you will explain yourself!" her mother said, voice elevated. "And if you raise your voice again, I can promise you that you will regret it. 'Honor thy mother.'"

Jezabel noted her mother had left out, "and thy father."

She didn't want trouble, so she silenced herself. She wouldn't scream, she wouldn't argue, but she wouldn't talk, either.

"Nothing to say?" her mother demanded.

Jezabel merely stood looking at the floor.

"Okay," said her mother, calmly. "Then you won't be getting this back."

Jezabel went into her yellow room, closed the door, sat on the edge of her bed and stared at the dirty, linoleum floor that should have been cream with a yellow throw rug but instead looked gray with a mud-streaked rag. She heard the sound of pages ripping and trash being collected. She heard the front door squeak open, and she heard the sound of a garbage can lid clunking. She heard a loud "thunk," and then the scraping sound of the lid being returned to its rightful place. The front door opened again, and she heard her mother running water in the kitchen.

That was the last time Jezabel ever had a private notebook or a picture of her father.

"Come on," he said, "do it. Do it!" He was panting from behind, grabbing painfully at her breasts. "You're all lubed, now," he grunted, "It won't hurt."

She shook her head no. But it was dark, and he couldn't see it.

"Come on!" he demanded, "Say you want me to do it. Say it."

"I don't want to," she whispered, barely audible.

She never could decide if he hadn't heard the "don't" or had just chosen to ignore it.

In an instant, he slid out from her, spread her buttocks and stabbed her. She knew she had screamed. She heard it from outside herself. She could feel herself sobbing from the pain that threatened to rip her in two. She heard his grunts and his demands to "take it, take it all." All she could do was wait for it to be over.

He finished. He fell asleep almost instantly.

She lay awake, eyes wide open, staring at her open bedroom

door. The door creaked and opened a little more. Tarika slinked into the room, quietly, not disturbing even a fiber on the rug. Tarika, her silent friend, Jezabel thought. The cat rubbed herself against the side of the bed and began to purr, silently, though Jezabel could feel the vibrations through her fingertips and up through the palms of her hands.

Hot tears had leaked from Jezabel's eyes and suddenly took a round, full form, lingering at the edge of her eyelashes and falling, falling from her to the bed, past the bed, onto Tarika's back. Jezabel thought the cat might run from the sense of water on her back, but instead, she rubbed harder against Jezabel's hand, refusing to leave.

Michael rolled over on the other side of the bed and both woman and cat froze, waiting.

He snorted and fell back to sleep.

She felt like she and Tarika exhaled at once.

Don't worry, Tarika, Jezabel thought. I'll never get rid of you. It doesn't matter what he says. He doesn't mean it. He doesn't mean half the things he says, she thought.

But didn't he? She wondered why he said those things, those things that really bothered her or why he hurt her and didn't stop. Didn't he know?

She blamed herself, telling herself and Tarika that she wasn't communicating well, that it was her fault and if she had the courage to say what had to be said, he would change and stop. But then she remembered some of the conversations where she did tell him things, told him clearly, she thought, and he didn't seem to care or he got mad. Was this how he was, or was this just how men were?

It was hard for her to know, never really living with a man. The couple of college boyfriends she had before were never serious. And she had never observed interactions between her father and her mother. She had only heard what her mother said about her father, and that certainly wasn't a good lesson in male/female communications.

She tried to understand relationships by looking at other people's relationships, but other than Michael's friend Tony, she didn't really know too many people in relationships. Charles was single, Tonya was divorced and Sharon...who would want to be in a relationship with Sharon anyway?

Michael, she thought, I don't understand you yet, but I am going to. Her anus throbbed. She picked up Tarika and hugged her.

At least we understand each other, Tarika, she thought. The cat purred and snuggled into Jezabel's arms.

Jezabel had been in college when her mother broke the news.

"I'm moving," her mother announced on the phone. "To Milwaukee."

Just like that.

"What?" Jezabel couldn't have been more taken off guard if her mother had told her she was getting remarried.

"Jezabel, I've been talking about it for awhile. You know how I feel about this area. And it's getting worse and worse."

Why Milwaukee, of all places? As far as Jezabel knew, they didn't have family out there. In fact, with the exception of distant cousins, they had no family left. Jezabel's grandparents had died, and her mother had estranged herself from Jezabel's father's side of the family long ago.

"Mom, it's the same place," Jezabel said. "It just has different people."

They were talking about the city again, her mother giving the familiar argument that the place was going downhill, that no one even spoke English anymore, that crime was everywhere and it just wasn't safe.

"Mom, that's how it is in every city. Don't you think you will get that in Milwaukee, too?"

"Your city is not the same place. It's more dangerous now. You shouldn't be living there either," her mother had told her. "Milwaukee is in the Midwest, much safer, fewer people, lower cost of living. And the police department already offered me the clerical job I applied for. Now all you have to do is get out, too, while you still can."

"Isn't that a little over dramatic, Mom?" she said, regretting the words as soon as they exited her unthinking mouth.

Jezabel heard that stubborn, low sigh her mother used just before she got angry. She wanted to diffuse it before it erupted like a dirty bomb.

"Mom," she said, "I can see why you might think that. But really, I'm perfectly safe here. The dorm is great, nice people, dorm supervisors, security guards...come on, you've been here."

The moment Jezabel said it, she felt an eye-twitch of guilt. She didn't particularly like the dorm crowds. Still, it was better than leaving the familiar environment.

"And I haven't been impressed, either," her mother said. "Those rooms are dingy, the windows are filthy. The last time I was there, your neighbors were throwing a beer party and the place smelled like smoke. I was told that was a no-smoking dorm. I don't know what is wrong with your dorm managers, but they obviously aren't doing their jobs."

Jezabel couldn't argue there. The dorm wasn't in the best shape. At least six or seven generations of college kids had lived in the refurbished warehouse—six or seven generations of partying, smoking and having sex in between the auspices of studying hard. It was expensive to live in a dorm, but it was even more expensive to live off campus, so Jezabel took what she could get. Besides, the meals were already paid. In the dorm, Jezabel could eat regularly and stick to the routine that helped her earn and maintain a 3.9 grade point average, an average that kept her in a constant flow of scholarships that paid for her room and board, such as it was. The plan was working. Why her mother wanted to disturb that, she didn't know.

But her mother was right about the dorm managers. They weren't exactly attentive. They closed their eyes to a lot of illicit behavior unless that behavior turned potentially violent or loud enough to attract the attention of the security guards. At least the dorm offered some kind of protection in that way.

"You can get a place out there, near me," her mother said. "You can rent a nice little room and get a little job out there. Do the college thing later or at night. It's cheaper in Milwaukee."

But even her mother didn't believe that one. Her mother knew she had her heart set on college, that she was a determined student, that she wanted to make something of herself, something more than a clerk or whatever her father had ended up doing, which might have been landing himself in jail. The idea of uprooting and moving with her mother was out of the question.

Besides, Jezabel had grown up in this area, knew nothing else and was too afraid to change. Her city provided a sense of comfort, a kind of teddy bear, even if it was a bear with patches and worn spots and one eye missing.

"But Mom," Jezabel said, starting to panic. "I haven't been here long enough to get an education that would let me get a decent job and pay for a security deposit, the plane ticket, food..."

"Jezabel, this is my decision," her mother said. "This isn't really up for discussion. You do what you want. You're an adult now.

"I already have a realtor. They have a buyer for me, and they have several homes for me to see. I've been telling you this for a long time—this is not news. My mind is made up. Now you need to make up yours."

"Mom," Jezabel said, starting to cry, "That's not fair! I mean, I'm in college. Why are you telling me this when I'm making it and doing well here? Where would I go over summer if I was out here alone? I can't stay in the dorm, and I wouldn't be able to afford to fly out every summer and you couldn't pay for my plane ticket. How can you do that?"

"Jezabel, I am being perfectly fair," her mother said, now in full-blown angry tone. "I've done everything for you. I've lived my whole life for you. I've taken care of you, gotten you through regular school, and now you are in college. You knew I couldn't afford to pay for your college, and I told you that at the start, that you would be on your own if you wanted college.

I have prayed for you more than daily, and I have had others pray for you, too. With the help of the Lord, I've raised you on my own, without your worthless thing called a father, without some man. You're doing well because everything I've invested in you, time and money. That's what I've done for you. And now that it's time for me to make a decision for me, you want to give me grief about it? Ha!"

Her mother had hung up. Jezabel sat in her room, staring at the telephone. It was like being back in her yellow room. She just sat and stared. But there were no cheery colored walls to make her feel better, and the stuffed kitty was stashed in the closet.

For a long time, she didn't let herself feel anything about her mother. She didn't want to hate her mother, not when she didn't have her father or really anyone else besides her college acquaintances. She could understand how her mother would want a place of her own and not be tied to some college kid who was just starting out. Her mother was getting older, and she wanted to live a few more years as an independent person, independent of having to take care of her.

Jezabel had worked hard and tried not to be an imposition, but she understood that just being there and needing to go back home on breaks and over the summer was a responsibility her mother didn't need or want at this time in her life and certainly not one her mother wanted in this city.

She remembered it all again, now on this Saturday morning, looking at Michael, drinking coffee and smoking a cigarette in her kitchen. "Hey, you wanna get together with Tony and Jen tonight?" he asked, taking a drag from the cigarette.

"Sure," she said.

Tony and Jen were old friends of Michael's. They had gone to high school together, and the other couple had been an item since the tenth grade. Tony and Michael occasionally worked jobs together, Tony working the inside wiring while Michael finished up siding and roofing. Jezabel liked to listen to the two of them banter stories back and forth about the other's ineptitude and sometimes, outright stupidity.

Jezabel looked forward to the evening even though she

wasn't really close to either Tony or Jen. It would be a diversion. But first, there was grocery shopping and planning to do. It looked like it would be a busy weekend. And Jezabel liked to be busy.

Chapter Seven

Jezabel couldn't help it. She was staring. The boy or the man, she wasn't sure which to call him, was talking to her. He was in his early twenties. And his tongue was forked. Literally.

He was telling her how he had a record and how hard it was to get a job. He liked to work and was good at detailing cars.

"No one cleans 'em up like I do," he said, his tongue flicking in an out, mesmerizing and horrifying at the same time.

Behind the fork flashed the gold bulb of a tongue ring. "I polish and clean and when the owners come back, they look at it like it's a new car. It looks new, too, 'cause I get the wheels and the rims and the inside. Smells new. They like that."

She remembered the advice Charles had given her, that she should do all the talking and not let them get a word in edgewise. But she had told him she couldn't possibly type and talk at the same time, and now she was once again proving that was true. She had tried with the last couple of clients and just ended up with a load of typos that slowed her down in the end. So now, she was typing, and the boy was talking and she was at least half-listening. She couldn't help it. At least when she was looking at the keyboard, she wasn't staring at his tongue.

From his neck down, he was covered in tattoos. All of snakes. Green snakes, purple snakes, red snakes, crawling from inside his nose, under his chin, down from the short sleeves of his purple t-shirt, through his fingers and up his forearm. She could picture the others, slithering their way down his stomach, past his belly button, towards…stop it!

Back to the tongue, which brought to mind some other images that made her have to turn her entire body away from the speaker.

She typed, trying to act normal. What the hell was she doing in this job, anyway? Oh yeah. She was stuck. That's right.

"So you use the leather cleaner all over the seats, even on the dashboard. But see that's how you can tell if it's a decent car. You use that cleaner on a cheap car and your dashboard ends up all streaky.

The good cars, you know the ones that cost some real bucks, they're all shiny and nice."

She nodded, and the boy/man shifted his weight, throwing his jeans jacket over the chair next to him. The jacked was painted in green, red and purple graffiti that she couldn't read.

She tried to picture him without the tattoos and the tongue stuff. He's probably pretty good looking, she thought. Actually, he was good looking anyway: dark hair, close cropped, blue-gray eyes that were more piercing than even his tongue ring, a broad smile and dimples. His jail story was mild compared to a few others she had heard. In a year for dealing at an early age, let out early for good behavior.

He had earned his GED while doing time, and he was out now, ready to work. Problem is, he had to work under the table. "Every time I apply somewhere and check off that little box that says I was a jailbird, I never get called," he said. "Keep telling my mom what the problem is, but she says it's cause of my tats. It ain't about my tats, though. I'm not dumb. I get it. Who wants to hire a con?"

She could tell he wasn't dumb by any stretch.

"You need your car detailed?"

She thought about her car, her car with the cracked dashboard, the filthy steering wheel, the more than one-hundred thousand miles that threatened to blow the engine at any point, and the way Michael sometimes drove the poor old thing like it was a race car or something. Of course, compared to his truck, yes, her car could make turns more quickly, and it had been known to run a yellow light or two, but not because it was a fast vehicle. It was a vehicle that had seen lots of use, some care, but a lot of activity that older cars just were not made for. Some day, she thought, she would get a newer car, one that didn't threaten to break down in the dead of winter or blow a tire on the highway just because something was wrong with the front end. Some day…

She was staring into space and remembered the boy, the boy with the forked tongue.

She wanted to laugh about the detailing offer but didn't because she didn't want him to think she was laughing at him. She looked at him, seriously, and said instead, "If you saw my car, you wouldn't be asking me that."

"That bad, huh?" he grinned. "What, don't you make the big bucks in a job like this?"

Now she did laugh. "Yeah, right. Listen, you're having a hard time getting a job, but trust me, it's bad all around. Just don't give up. You'll get something else eventually."

Why she felt the need to give him this advice, she didn't know. Maybe it was that she needed to actually believe what she was saying. Again, she told herself to stop it, not to get personal with these people, not to let them get to her like this. In spite of Charles's advice, she realized the less she said to them, the better off they all would be. Who knew what might come out of her own mouth? Better to let it come out of theirs and just ignore it. Bobby and John would have told her the same thing.

She remembered Bobby and John were due in today. She had arrived early after her weekend with Michael. She had dressed in her navy suit, something she hardly ever did if she could help it because the last thing she wanted was to resemble Sharon in any way. Of course, it was a cheap suit, one of only two she owned, so she had little to worry about in terms of really copying Sharon. Jezabel had purchased the suit at the same thrift shop where she got her furniture and silverware, but still, the suit was dressier than she was used to. Besides, she cringed at the idea of having to dress up just because she knew the big bosses would be in. It felt hypocritical.

"Let me get some copies for you," she told the boy.

At this point, looking at his hair and his snakes and his jacket again and thinking about him living with his mother, she decided he was, indeed, still a boy in a lot of ways, a boy who just happened to be old enough to have been sent to a jail for adults. The short hair and the jail thing had given him an air of experience and maturity, but the rest...and compared to Michael...

Michael again, she thought, as she made her copies and listened to the rhythm of Tonya answering the phone and Charles reciting his spiel to his client. The weekend had been okay. They talked about Michael giving notice to his landlord and moving out by the middle of next month. Tony and Jen had come over, and Michael explained about the truck, that he was going to get that motorcycle even though Tony said it was a bad idea.

Jezabel had wanted to know earlier how Michael was going to buy the motorcycle, but he wouldn't discuss it other than to say there were places out there just dying to give people like him loans. Jezabel knew all about those places. She worked for one.

Tony and Jen had stayed a few hours, the four of them drinking beers and literally giggling over a stupid movie they had rented and brought over, something about killer paper dolls that came to life.

"This is great," Tony said. "It just doesn't get any better than this, does it, Mikey? Remember all that time and money we used to waste in the bar?" he asked. "Tell you what, nothing like hanging with good friends and laughing. Glad you two finally decided to cohabitate, as they say," he said raising his beer bottle. "Here's to the love birds!"

They all drank to Michael and Jezabel. Jezabel screwed up her face. She didn't really like beer, but she sipped it to be sociable. She preferred sweet mixed drinks that didn't taste like alcohol, but she couldn't afford the ingredients, and even if she could, she wouldn't know how to prepare them. So beer had to suffice on a Saturday night with a stupid movie. She was enjoying it anyway.

Tony was the consummate gentleman, opening Jen's beer, offering her a comfy seat next to him, putting his arm around her and patting her on the head now and then. When he got up, he offered Jen and everyone else another drink, something she was almost sure Michael had never done. She wished some of Tony's manners and good nature would rub off on Michael, so whenever he suggested the two couples get together, she always said yes. Besides, Jen was very sweet, even though Jezabel didn't have much in common with her.

"I can help you unpack," Jen offered. "It sucks trying to unpack on your own. I know when I moved my things into Tony's it was a drag, and I didn't even have all the stuff Michael has. You have to figure out how all that crap is going to fit with yours, like his kitchen things. You won't want to have too many duplicates, but it'll be good because he has stuff you don't have and you put them together, and it's a whole lot of stuff. But you have to figure out how to get it all in and organized."

If Jen didn't live in the city and hadn't completed some college, Jezabel might have mistaken her for a country girl with minimal education.

"Hey, thanks Jen," Jezabel said. "I really appreciate that. I've been trying to figure out what we'll do if we have double stuff."

"Easy," said Michael and laughed. "We throw your junk out!" He slapped his knee. "Including that damn cat!"

"Hey, that ain't nice, man," Tony said. "You want this to work, you gotta give and take, you know?"

"Yeah, yeah," Michael said. "I know. I'm just kidding." He took a swig of his beer. "But I'm not kidding about that cat. God I hate that bitch."

"What wrong with cats?" Tony asked. "I think cats are cool. They're kind of like women. You know...they only want you when they want you but when the do want you, well then man, look out!"

Jen hit him in the stomach playfully.

"See what I mean?" he said. "They'll fight you all the way, but when it comes down to it, they really love you even if they pretend they don't."

Jen shook her head. "Don't worry. I'll help you," Jen said again to Jezabel who looked worried now in spite of the other couple's fun. "We'll figure it out. Your place is big enough."

A thin brunette, Jen worked as a cashier in a busy department store, had worked there for several years, moving from general clerk to cashier to supervisor. She had lots of regular customers and lots of patience. Jezabel liked that about Jen and liked to hear the ways that Jen had learned to deal with difficult customers. She had taken some of Jen's advice back to the office with her, and now, thinking about their weekend, she reminded herself to tell Jen about the boy with the forked tongue.

What would Jen do with him? And what would ever possess anyone to split his own tongue, Jezabel wondered.

She walked back into her office and handed snake-boy his paperwork.

"Okay," she said, showing him where to sign. "There are a few things I have to say to make this a valid contract."

She caught herself over-explaining the agreement again, a no-no according to Bobby and John. The last thing they wanted was one of their employees giving the clients more information that could make them change their minds at the last moment. Just recite the disclaimer. No more, no less.

"Remember, In-a-Pinch is not a bank. You are taking out a high interest loan to be repaid over a six-month period."

The boy looked worried. She stopped, wondering if he wanted to say anything, but he remained silent. "You will be responsible for the principal of the loan, monthly interest accrued at 27% and the initiation fee of $75.00. If you miss one or more payments," she continued.

He did interrupt her. "You think I'll be able to pay this off?" he asked.

"Well, um, I mean," she said.

What was she supposed to say to him?

"I mean, you just went through the whole thing," she said. "You said you were going to get some more cars to detail, right?" she asked.

Now she was nervous. She hated this. She knew the collections rate, and she knew she had told him the risks and he had still accepted. It wasn't her job to advise him, was it? No. It was her job to make loans and let the customers leave all happy and relieved that they could pay off their bills for the moment. That was her job. That's it, she reminded herself.

"But, what if I don't get the cars?" he asked.

"Okay, look," she said, regrouping. "I mean, if you are that worried, do you want to take some time to think about it? I can hold your paperwork if you want."

"You know, that might be a good idea," the boy said.

The crease in his young forehead disappeared. He exhaled. "I think I should do that, you know. I've really been trying not to make snap decisions lately. That's what got me into trouble in the first place, you know, not paying attention to what I was doing to get money, not caring and I can't do that anymore, no matter how broke I am." She nodded. "So, thanks. I really appreciate that."

Snake-boy grabbed his coat. A pack of cigarettes fell out of his pocket. She wanted to tell him he could save lots of money and his lungs if he quit smoking, but she resisted the urge. She wasn't his mother. He had a mother! And his mother didn't like his tattoos, which also must have cost a fortune.

"Thanks," he said. "So should I call you and let you know?"

She didn't have a card. Bobby and John didn't give the reps cards. The only calls came through Tonya. That's how they wanted it. Cards made the clients feel like they had reps who had time and ambition to work closely with them. It wasn't that kind of business. It wasn't personal.

"Just call the main number," Jezabel said. "Ask for me. Tonya can put you through. Or come back in. It's up to you."

The boy stood up and offered Jezabel a handshake. "Thanks," he said. "I'll give you a call."

The boy walked through the door, nearly colliding with two men standing outside. "Excuse me," the boy said. The men stepped into the office.

Bobby and John were dressed in their usual expensive suits. "Jezabel!" Bobby said, his blond hair slicked back, smile covering his face like wallpaper. "How are you?"

Jezabel jumped. She hadn't seen or heard them outside her office. And her client that hadn't signed just walked right past them. She wanted to smack her own forehead. What an idiot she was!

"Good," she said, extending her hand to shake Bobby's instead of hitting herself. His hand was cold and rough, but clean with manicured nails, like he had done manual work at some point but had given it up.

"Mind if we sit down?" John asked, sitting before she answered.

John looked at her directly. He wasn't smiling. He was the one who never bothered with niceties. Good cop, bad cop.

"We just bumped into one of your clients," John said. "One of your clients who didn't sign the agreement."

"I know," she said quickly. "It's the first one I've ever had who didn't sign immediately," she explained. Her hands threatened to start shaking. She put them quickly on her lap.

"You know what you did wrong?" he asked. He picked up a pencil from her desk and started tapping it, a regular, rhythmic beat.

"I'm not sure," she lied.

Bobby smiled, "Now come on, John," he said. "Can't blame a girl for being nice, right? Isn't that what we like about girls?"

"Right," said John. "You can be nice," he paused and stopped tapping, leaning over the desk, looking Jezabel in the face, "but make sure they sign."

Jezabel averted her eyes and nodded silently.

"If they've gotten through the whole thing and come down to signing, they want the loan. You get the signature and they leave happy. That's it. That's all there is to it. I know you know this."

Jezabel nodded again, silent.

"You don't give them options or reasons or explanations. And you don't listen to their sob stories. That's not what we hire you to do. You aren't a counselor. You give them the loan and you explain policy. No more. You understand?" John said quietly.

Jezabel nodded and looked at him so he would know she was listening.

He had thin lips that stretched to taut lengths when he smiled, the kind of smile that looked like it took a lot of effort to produce and so when he did, you somehow owed him for making the attempt.

"Yes," she said. "I'm sorry. I'm usually better at that. I don't know what happened just then. Guess I was just kind of…"

Bobby shook his head, "No apology necessary, Jezabel. We know you've had a practically perfect client record. We know you can get them in and set up just fine. You're dependable and we know you do your job well. Just don't let it happen again."

Bobby's smile was less forced. It was the natural, practiced smile of someone who smiled a lot because it was his job to look happy and positive, but still, most anyone could tell from the lines near his dark eyes that he was capable of much more than smiling. What else he was capable of, Jezabel didn't want to know.

"I won't," she said, grateful for Bobby's friendlier tone, no matter what lived behind it. John simply scared the wits out of her.

"So anyway, the real reason we came her," Bobby continued, "is to tell you we've decided this place needs an official manager." His smile spread wider, if that was possible. His eyes focused on her intently, making her uncomfortable. She held his gaze for a moment, almost fascinated by his expression, but then looked down at her desk.

"Oh!" Jezabel said.

Uh-oh, she thought. Were they bringing someone in from the outside, someone new? Or were they...

For a second, she wondered if they were going to offer her the job. After all, she had been here long enough, had a good record that they noticed and did have some education behind her. She didn't know if she wanted the position, but she knew she was qualified for it, and the extra money would be great on top of having Michael move in and help with the bills. But no. She wasn't aggressive enough. And that meant...

Her mind took off, in time for John to say, "So starting today, Sharon Stuart is the new Office Manager."

Jezabel sat silent clamping her jaws together so they didn't fall open into a horrified gape. She wasn't surprised this was going to happen, but she still felt like someone wearing boxing gloves had punched her in the face.

Both men looked at her, raising their eyebrows, waiting for a response.

"Oh, um, well, that's great!" Jezabel said, trying to sound bright and positive. "I'll be sure to congratulate her," she said, hurriedly. "Sharon, um, she knows what she's doing," Jezabel trailed off.

"We thought you'd say that," John said. "We'll make the formal announcement this afternoon, so you can hold the congratulations until then. We'll all meet in her office at 2:00."

"Okay," Jezabel said. "Okay."

The men got up. "We're heading into Charles's now," they said. "Tonya already knows, and Sharon knows, so it's no secret. See you at 2:00."

Jezabel managed another atrophied smile.

She felt like she was going to throw up.

Tony and Jen had left, and Jezabel and Michael had gone to bed. Michael had propped himself up on his elbows, looking at her. "Let's have a baby," he said.

"Right now?" she laughed, kidding.

"Yeah, right now."

"Right this minute?"

"No, not right the minute, stupid," he said. "You go off the pill. Then we'll have a baby."

"Isn't this a bit premature?" she asked, still light and kidding.

"I mean, you haven't even moved your stuff in yet."

"So by the time I move my stuff in, you can be off the pill and we can be making a baby."

She sat up. "You're serious, aren't you?"

"Yeah, I'm serious, why?"

"Michael! We haven't even done the move-in thing and already you're talking about having a baby. Don't you think that's a little..."

He rolled over, away from her. "Forget it," he said. "Forget I said anything about it, okay?"

"Well, no, Michael, it's not that, it's just that the last thing I expected was you to ask me to have a baby. I mean, our jobs are so..."

"So what?" he asked, flipping back around, facing her, angry. "What? What about our jobs?"

"Well I mean, you aren't working right now..."

"Oh so that's it," he demanded. "I'm not working right now so that makes me some kind of loser. Doesn't matter that my job starts next week or that me moving in here is going to save your poor ass..."

"What?" she asked, sitting up. "What? Wait a minute...where did that come from?" Her tone had been louder than usual. That's how shocked she was that he would even say that.

"Forget it. Just forget it!" he said. He threw the covers off and grabbed his jeans from the floor, pulling them up.

"What are you doing?" she asked, incredulous that this conversation had started at all, that it had actually taken place and had gone in this direction. "Michael, don't be silly. Let's talk..."

"Nope. I ain't talking," he said, heading for the bedroom door.

"Where are you going?" she asked.

"Out," he said, and she heard the front door slam.

She had flopped back against her pillow. What was wrong with that man?

First he wants to have a baby, then he accuses her of asking him to move in and for the sole reason that she didn't have enough money. As if she had suggested it to him! As if she were the one not working steadily!

Sure, she knew things were tough at work. She didn't make a lot of money, it was true, but she did work full time. She had health insurance and she managed to pay her bills, so long as she didn't spend any more than she had to on household and food items. How dare he?

She had been so angry, she didn't know what else to do, so she cried, for the second time that weekend. This was ridiculous. Stupid. Why was she even bothering with him and this move?

She remembered the girls in the dorm. They would have said to dump him as soon as he was jobless, which he had been just six months into their relationship because his contract ended. But what would they know about contract work and real labor anyway? Some of them had never had to work. Their parents put them through school, they had mothers and fathers, and they didn't have to worry the same way Jezabel did. Besides, that was a long time ago, and those girls didn't matter anymore. They were probably married and divorced since then, anyway.

Jezabel had pulled the covers over her eyes.

She must have fallen asleep, because she didn't hear Michael come through the door. He slid into bed and kissed her. "I'm sorry babe," he said. "I'm really sorry. I lost my head and...I'm sorry." He smelled like beer. But he didn't sound drunk or angry the way he did when he really did a lot of drinking. So she had accepted the apology and a hug that lasted into a long holding and ended up with them gently making love. They had both fallen asleep, exhausted.

The next morning, she called her mother, but no one answered. Jezabel guessed her mother was at church.

She didn't leave a message.

Chapter Eight

She knew that she needed a walk in the park after work. She looked forward to it, like visiting an old friend who always seemed to be there when you needed her the most. Or maybe it was the bunnymoose who was her friend. Pretty sad when your closest friend in an imaginary creature, she thought.

One minute before her shift ended, she was putting on her coat and heading for the door. She didn't care if Sharon noticed or if Sharon even existed. She had to get out of that place.

Tonya was on the phone and waved Jezabel out the door, giving her a sympathetic look. They had all been giving each other those looks since this morning's visits and the fateful 2:00 meeting. At the meeting, the three of them had nodded brief congratulations to Sharon. Then Charles looked at Jezabel and rolled his eyes. Jezabel was certain John saw him do it. But Charles wouldn't care.

"Let me tell you something," Charles had said to her, "I don't let no thug, no matter how good he dresses, intimidate me." He meant it.

The bus screamed up to the corner a couple of minutes later, and Jezabel didn't even bother trying to find a seat. A good crowd was riding this afternoon, and she actually preferred to stand, even if it did mean occasionally being bumped by the succession of mostly teens and workers coming on at the end of the day. A burly, curly haired worker in a thick, corduroy jacket jostled her and turned to say, "Hey, sorry." He paused, seeming to briefly admire her eyes, but Jezabel was too tired, too preoccupied to acknowledge it or care.

She often wondered why she felt a disconnect between her outer self and her inner self, her external shell that seemed to exude a kind of beauty and attraction that her mind and heart never fully absorbed. She knew she was pretty, but she didn't feel pretty, or at least she thought she didn't feel pretty. She thought she knew what pretty people who felt pretty actually did feel like, and she knew she wasn't it. She always seemed to have this kind of self-inflicted prison that didn't allow her to enjoy being looked at or admired or acknowledged as being attractive. She kept her feelings of being pretty walled up, along with the words she never dared exhale at work, to Michael or to her mother.

She never did anything really to call attention to herself or her looks. She didn't wear much makeup, if any, did hardly anything with her long, straight hair and paid minimal attention to her cheap clothing. Jezabel didn't go out of her way to dress sexy, even for Michael who had asked her several times to wear lingerie or a short skirt that he said would look hot on her shapely legs. When she wasn't in office appropriate pants and a sweater, she mostly wore jeans and sweatshirt. In the summer, she wore Bermuda shorts and sandals, and while she did wear a two piece bathing suit the rare occasions they went to the beach or swimming, it was the kind that looked like a jogging suit with shorts. No one could ever say that Jezabel was vain.

In fact, she wondered if anyone could really say anything about her at all. She thought about the people who might claim to know her, what they actually knew about her and what that would mean. Of course Michael knew all about her family and her job, and Charles and Tonya knew about Michael, and her mother knew about Jezabel's formative years, and there were Jen and Tony and a few of other people like cops that she bumped into in the street, but all in all, Jezabel had the uncanny feeling that no one really knew her, all of her. She relished that feeling, protected it and hated it all at once. In the middle of the jerking bus, holding onto the cold bar, she sighed and fleetingly wondered if anyone could hear her.

The feeling took her down the stairs and toward the park, through the arch of the entrance where no homeless man hovered this time. But when she reached the circle with the benches, she did notice a man in a long, dusty looking black coat, ragged khaki pants and a thick wool hat, lying on the left bench. The hat was pulled over his eyes, and three sheets of newspaper barely clung to the length of his fetal-positioned body. Jezabel wondered if the man had been reading the newspaper or was trying to use the thin pages as covers.

She took her usual route to the little woods, not caring how many homeless men might be camping there or whether or not some mystical creature awaited, eager to pounce on her and her funk. Her world couldn't get much heavier than it was now, she thought, so what was one more weird event in the life of a nobody that nobody knew or cared to know? She could be homeless herself. What would that be like? Maybe it would be better, living day to day in a park visited by hoards of bunnymoose.

She stopped in front of the little, rickety fence and briefly wondered if it had been longer and better built at some other time, if it was meant to keep people out or other things in. Things like what, she asked herself. Things like bunnymoose? She might have laughed at herself except that she wasn't in a laughing mood. She might have cried, but she couldn't.

And she might have been surprised when she heard the familiar rustle of the underbrush just beyond the landmark rock, but she wasn't. She waited because she knew what she would see next — the furry legs and hooves of a creature she had witnessed only once before but had come there seeking again only to be disappointed. Even so, somehow, she knew she would see it again. It wasn't her imagination. She decided to believe that.

Part by part, as was its way, the bunnymoose appeared, first the legs, then the chest, then the nose with its oddly elongated whiskers, then the forehead and bits of the long, floppy ears. The neck and huge shoulders came through slowly, woods groaning in labor, delivering next the creature's back, belly and buttocks before the rear legs and tail appeared.

Jezabel noticed the tail this time, a kind of mangy looking thing, like Tarika's tail after she had run through her cat pan and then rolled around the apartment. Leaves and brush and some drying mud clung to the tail, and Jezabel wondered if there were more than just mud there. The thing was obviously an animal, and in the absence of a place to bathe, there probably wasn't much the bunnymoose could do with the dirtier aspects of animalhood, things she and Michael sometimes referred to as "cling-ons."

She looked into the orbs of the beast and wondered briefly if the bunnymoose ever went to the little overflow pond to bathe, or if it stayed in its woods, covered in brush and trees and privacy. She waited for the thing to stop walking, the way it did before, but it didn't. It came closer to Jezabel.

It was heading straight for her.

Jezabel might have turned to run if she hadn't been more than amazed and paralyzed by the sheer height of the thing — she still didn't know what it was or if it were dangerous or if it were real. No wait. She had decided it was indeed real. This thing must be real. And it was coming over to check her out.

It stopped just in front of the little fence, as if it had this strange sense of personal space that it respected, even though it could have easily trampled the fence.

It looked down at her, cocking its head, its huge ears brushing the top of the fence.

Jezabel looked into its eyes and just stood like that.

"Hello," she said.

And while she was aware the thing wasn't moving its mouth, it talked to her. In her head.

"Hello," it said.

"What are you?" she asked.

"Oughtn't you ask how are you?" the bunnymoose asked her.

"Oh. I'm sorry. It's been a terribly long day. How are you?"

"I am well, and I am timeless," it said.

Jezabel paused. She was reminded of Alice in Wonderland, but for some reason, the whole things felt normal to her. Maybe that's how Alice had felt, too.

"Well, I feel timeless," she said, "and I am not sure I like how it feels. It makes me feel old."

"It's doesn't matter how it feels," said the bunnymoose in her head. "It just is."

Jezabel thought about that and didn't say anything.

"If we went all the time by our feelings, we would never have made it to where we are now," the bunnymoose said. "And if we made decisions based only on our intellect, the same thing would happen."

"What is that?" she asked.

"You already know."

She inhaled the idea and the creature's voice. It was a low voice, a deep voice, male and female at the same time, resonating and peaceful like water and wind and perfume. She thought its voice would sound more awe-inspiring, like God's from a burning bush, but it didn't. It sounded natural, part of her, like her whole body was feeling the voice from her head through her veins. She breathed it again and again.

"Do you have anything else?" the bunnymoose asked.

"Anything else?" she said. "What do you mean?"

"Anything else you want to ask?"

She had a million questions, at least, but at the moment, she couldn't think of a single one. It was like her thoughts had been erased, leaving only her body and senses.

She shook her head.

The bunnymoose twitched its large, wet and soft looking nose, bowed its furry head, and offered her itself to her touch.

As if gravity didn't exist, her fingers floated to the bridge of the creature's nose and ran from between the huge eyes and down to the nostrils. The hair felt fine and coarse at the same time, neither bunny nor moose. And definitely not human.

It nodded at her and turned to go.

"What are you?" she called to it, not wanting to let it leave without having at least that question answered.

The thing turned its head back. "I'm a bunnymoose, of course."

And it made its way back into its woodsy home.

She sat at her kitchen table, alone with her hot tea, the cat on her lap and the picture of the creature in her mind. What a bizarre way to spend an evening, she thought...sitting here alone, petting a pretty, purring thing and thinking about something that didn't exist, because back in the real world, she decided that the thing wasn't real after all. She supposed it was better than the way she had spent the rest of the day, however. And she was too tired to wonder if she were really going insane or if she had mental health benefits.

The 2:00 meeting had been more than just horrible. Sharon obscured her gloating face with the demure half smile of a professional accustomed to succeeding. That she worked in a cruddy little building for lecherous lenders didn't seem to make any difference to her. That her soon-to-be underlings hated her didn't seem to phase her, either. She appeared oblivious to everything except the lauding of first, the understated John, and then, the boisterous Bobby. The men's gold rings gleamed as they clapped their hands in appreciation of their new star employee, and the three others felt forced to do something similar.

After the men left, Charles and Jezabel walked as normal back to their offices, and Tonya back to the front desk. Sharon made a personal appearance to each of them, simpering that she so appreciated their enthusiasm and she looked forward to working with them as a unified group. "Together, I am sure we can make, meet and exceed our goals," she said, her voice rising a bit, her pronunciation even more heightened, as if she had turned from loan shark rep to great orator. Sharon really did believe all the stuff that came out of her prim, irritating mouth. "We can overachieve, I know it, and in the wake of increased revenue..."

That's about where Jezabel stopped listening and just watched Sharon's lips moving, those cracking, dry lips that faked smiles, hinted, insinuated and probably outright lied. Her skin had started to wrinkle, and the makeup didn't do a very good job of hiding the fact that Sharon was aging.

The orange-tinted lipstick made Sharon even uglier, though her face wasn't the worst looking one Jezabel had ever seen, especially considering some of the clients that came begging. Jezabel decided it was Sharon's attitude, her air of haughty superiority, her conviction in the higher power of the company structure and her unwillingness to see herself as anything other than a pawn of Bobby and John's rapacious business practices that made her uglier than a predator.

When had she come to this realization? She guessed it was recently. Jezabel had worked there long enough to see it all and too much of it. She had ignored it, for the most part, but it had been difficult, and lately, impossible. And after Sharon's promotion, she knew it would be harder and harder to dismiss the rumors, a now and then ragged client coming in with a final payment, a client that didn't look that ragged the first time, but looked more under the weather now, sickly, and in some cases, bruised.

Jezabel didn't see it too often because most of the time, delinquent clients settled the account outside the office doors. But on a couple of occasions, as she stood at the copier, she watched a client that she had processed limp through the door and place a money order in front of Tonya who stopped whatever she was doing, logged into the client's account, noted the payment and quickly sent the client back on his or her way. The last thing Tonya needed in the lobby was "exhibit A" of In-a-Pinch's collection techniques.

It was another reason Jezabel didn't want to remember her client's names, didn't want to get personally involved with them and didn't spend a lot of time in the lobby other than to make her copies, print and stretch her cramped legs. She just couldn't take one more thing to feel bad about. Little by little, comment by comment, Tonya and Charles and Bobby and John said things that made Jezabel understand collections was not a nice process.

And she wasn't sure it was an entirely legal process, either. It worried her. She didn't know if she should outright ask Tonya or Charles, or if she should just pretend she knew nothing. She decided on pretending ignorance if for no other reason than she really didn't know what was going on, it didn't affect her job directly and she didn't want to end up as someone who knew "too much." While Jezabel was not prone to dramatics, she was intelligent and pragmatic — she worked in a city with a high crime rate and a large population of poor. And given her own life experiences, she knew that things didn't always operate the way the law or the majority expected they would. Better she just keep out of it, keep her job and keep quiet.

She commended herself on doing a pretty good job until lately, especially until now. Now, for whatever reason, she felt like everything was coming to a head, like a wave peaking to a crest — and she was about to drown in it.

She took a sip of the hot tea and stroked Tarika's ear. Tarika purred. Lovely kitty, she thought. I don't care what Michael says. You aren't going anywhere.

Michael. He hadn't actually said a word about the cat again, and Jezabel was surprised. Maybe he had just forgotten. Tarika had taken off the last time he was here, hid somewhere until all the fighting and love making were over. Once he was gone, she came back out, jumped into bed with Jezabel, and replaced Michael, lying contented on his pillow. Jezabel giggled. Michael would have had a fit for sure.

The phone rang, and Jezabel wondered if she should even get it. After three rings, she sighed, got up and said "hello."

"Jezabel?" It was Michael. "Hey, look, I have some bad news."

She sat down. He had to be kidding. Bad news? What more bad news could there be after a day like this?

"God, this sucks," he said. "I am so fucking pissed, I just can't deal. You know that job I was supposed to start today?"

"Yes," she said quietly. She thought she should feel something, some more kind of foreboding, but curiously, she felt nothing.

"Well, I go to the site today, right. I had to take a cab because my truck is dead and I don't have the bike yet. So I get over there and the foreman says, 'Hey, where's your truck?' So I tell him. So you know what the fucker says? 'Well sorry man, can't use you then.' So I say, 'Whaddaya mean you can't use me? You said you could use me last week,' and he says, 'Yeah but you said you had a truck. You need to be bringing stuff back and forth, I need you hauling. Can't use you without wheels, man.' I wanted to punch the mother fucker in the face but what the fuck could I do?"

Jezabel sat in silence.

"You there?" he asked.

"Yes," she said quietly. "I'm listening."

"So he says he might have something for me in a couple of weeks, something that doesn't require hauling, but right now, for right now…" Michael paused. He actually sounded panicked. "Right now, he's got nothing for me."

"Michael, what are you going to do?" she asked.

She was trying to focus, trying to make herself feel something other than just a heavy weight, sitting in a cheap chair in an apartment, a heavy, voiceless, numb weight.

"Shit, I don't know. I know I already gave my notice here, so he's going to expect something before I leave, last month's rent or something or maybe he'll just use my security deposit, but shit, I don't know. I don't have any money to get the truck out, can't sell it, and now I don't have a job, so it's going to be kind of hard to go in and get a loan for the motorcycle. Shit, I don't know. You got any ideas? Got any money?" he asked.

She said nothing. She had lent him the last bit she could stretch out without going into debt herself. There was nothing left. That's how she felt, like there was nothing left to the little bit she considered hers. She had dissolved.

"Guess not," he said, since she said nothing. "Hell, I don't know. I'll figure it out. Just start packing my stuff and try to get something else. You mind if I use your car for a couple of weeks?"

"No, I don't mind," she said. And she really didn't. She didn't feel anything, so why should she mind?

"Can you come over and get me and I'll drop you back off? I'm going to need it tomorrow to take care of some things."

"Sure," she said. "I'll be right over."

She hung up the phone, put on her shoes and grabbed her keys. It was late, and she had to be up early in the morning. But it didn't seem to matter.

Like the bunnymoose said. If she went by how she felt—or in this case, didn't feel—she wouldn't do anything ever again.

"Don't you ever date or marry someone like your father."

Her mother had said that since she was ten years old, before she even thought about dating, before she had learned what she later considered the gory facts of life, before she had ever kissed a guy or even wanted to.

She recalled that first kiss. What was his name? Alexander? Albert? Alien? Something that started with an "A." The thing she actually recalled was the way his tongue swiped across her front teeth again and again. When he pushed it into her mouth, she almost gagged. His tongue felt like something that belonged at the bottom of a pond. She had fresh breath, but he tasted like the bologna sandwiches her mother made her in elementary school.

Was Alexander/Albert anything like her father? She couldn't really say. She didn't know her father, and she didn't know the kisser very well. He was a blind date a high school friend had set her up with. Jezabel wondered what had happened to her friend—Theresa was her name. They lost touch when Jezabel went to college.

"Your father was a drunk, a waster of God's resources (Jezabel didn't know if her mother meant ducks or money) and a rotten father."

Jezabel had nodded, a silent promise, just to shut her mother up.

She pulled up to Michael's apartment house. The driveway was black, the porch light out again. She had been here in the dark enough to have memorized the steps up to the door, feel her way into the front hall, and up the steep, wooden staircase to his apartment. She was too feeling-less to fear anything anyway.

"How are you doing?" a voice said.

She jumped enough to drop the keys.

"Hey, sorry," the voice said. "Didn't mean to startle you."

She squinted in the dark and recognized the voice and frame of Michaels' neighbor, the one she thought was gay.

"Oh, good, good," she said. "Whew, you scared me," she laughed nervously but sincerely.

"I know. Sorry," he said. He reached down, felt around the ground, and handed her the keys. "Damn landlord lets this light go out all the time. Dangerous, you know? You be careful on those steps, now."

"I will," she said. "Thanks."

He followed her in as far as the foyer and then went his own way.

Something about him made Jezabel want to stop and talk more. Irrationally, she wanted to spill her guts to him. She wanted to cry and tell him about work and Bobby and John and Sharon getting promoted and her terrible job and Michael losing his job and not having enough money and how she knew she was losing her mind because, had he ever been to Felonias Park? Had he ever seen it, that thing, that thing with the head of a lop-eared rabbit and the body of a moose? No? Would he want to come with her some time and see if it appeared, just so she would know she wasn't crazy? She would really like that. She could really use a friend.

With a sad shake of her head, she realized she was once again carrying on conversations in her mind, this time with a man she hardly knew. But, she thought, at least she knew he existed, which was more than she could say for that bunnymoose thing.

She knocked on Michael's door.

"Hey," he said. "Come on in."

His apartment looked like a real moose had traipsed through it. Clothes were strewn throughout the living room in piles, a hill of broken boxes sat in the corner. By the window snaked cords and wires apparently attached to a broken down stereo system that Jezabel couldn't tell if he was trying to repair or dismantle or ready for sale. It looked like he had started some packing. She saw three dishes and two glasses in a box on the kitchen table, and the refrigerator was open. Nothing was in it except beer, and Michael had been in the process of throwing away old jars of molding things like jellies and relish when he apparently decided to use up some of the beer.

"Hey," she said. She handed him the keys.

"Hey, well, I'd ask if you wanted to stay over here, but it's kind of a wreck," he said. "I started to…" he gestured.

"Yeah," she nodded. "Let's just go. I'm real tired."

"Okay," he said, and they went back to her car.

The seats were cold by that time, and they drove back in silence. She wondered if he thought she was mad at him, if he even cared if she was mad, or if he was so caught up in his anger that he had thought she might have an opinion over him being jobless again. Or still jobless. Whichever.

She looked at his profile. He was so good looking, but she couldn't see it right now. Not that he looked ugly or anything, but he seemed to fall into that big pit of nothingness that had attacked her in the night. She didn't like the nothing, but she didn't didn't like it enough to hate it, so she just accepted the fact that at this very moment, she was not attracted to Michael in the least.

If he wanted to make love, she wondered if she could even do it. Well that was ridiculous, she thought, because sometimes, she didn't feel like doing it but she did it anyway because…

Because, why? Because she felt like she had to? Because she felt like he would be mad if she said no? Because she was worried if she said no she would lose him? Because if she said no, he would do it anyway? She might have stopped herself from this train of thought, but since she had no feelings attached to it, she just kept going. What would he do?

She remembered one night when he had been drinking and she told him no. It was the night he had come banging on her door, demanding to be let in. She wouldn't let him in and when she finally did (because she was afraid her invisible neighbors would call the police and he would be arrested), he lunged at her, grabbing her shoulders, and pushed her down on the couch. She told him to stop and he didn't. He was mad and he kept saying, "What's the matter? Don't you want me? Huh, don't you want me?"

She told him no, not like this, and he ripped the shoulder of her shirt down, tearing her bra away and bit her breast, hard. He unbuttoned her pants and raked them down her legs, did the same with his pants and jammed himself inside her without even removing her panties. He panted, humping her, saying, "What's the matter? Don't you want me? Huh? Don't you want this?"

She was crying and shaking her head. He was hurting her, but he didn't stop. He didn't stop, and she remembered looking at him in that same way she looked at him now, like he was someone who seemed like he should be good looking but wasn't in the least.

He brought the car into the lot of her apartment buildings, and she got ready to get out. She didn't know if she should ask him to stay over or not. They hadn't been in the habit of staying at each other's places in the middle of the week, but lately, things hadn't been usual. He looked at her, so she asked. "Did you want to stay over or did you want to go back to your place?"

"Think I'll go back to my place and do some more cleaning up," he said.

"Okay, I'll talk to you tomorrow." She got out of the car.

No kiss or anything. She wondered when that had started. They used to kiss all the time. Now she felt like he kissed her only when he wanted to have sex, and even then...

Forget it, she told herself. Go to bed.

She did.

The phone rang. It was 3:00 a.m. "What, Michael?" she asked.

"Can I come over?"

"Michael I have to work tomorrow and I have all this crap going on at work."

"So the answer is no," he said. He sounded mad. Oh no. Was he drunk?

"Michael, have you been drinking?" she asked.

"Little," he said. "Not much."

"Michael, I have to get some sleep. Can we talk tomorrow?"

"Yeah. Sure. We can talk tomorrow," he said, and he hung up.

Jezabel unplugged the phone and fell right back to sleep.

Chapter Nine

The man leaned over, practically folding himself in half to reach the ties of his shoes. The shoes themselves had the look of faded black suede that had been cleaned too often. On one side, a piece of tape poked through a hole that had been patched. The laces had started to fray, the plastic ends long since replaced by knots preventing the laces from slipping through. The man straightened. Jezabel walked in, just in time for her to have seen the shoe tying.

"Sorry for the delay," she said, hanging up her coat. "It's been a crazy morning."

"Judging from the crowd in the lobby, I can see that," the man said. He wore a tweed jacket with worn spots at the elbows, a wrinkled, navy blue shirt underneath and navy colored trousers. Jezabel immediately thought "trousers" and not "pants" after hearing the man speak.

There was something regal, educated or dignified about his speech, the tone of his voice and words he chose, not in that overly-enunciated way Sharon had, but in the way that says the speaker had gone through several years of college. Jezabel would have bet he graduated and even earned advanced degrees. She wished she had done half so much.

Sharon's first day on the job as supervisor, and already she was raising her eyebrow, looking at the clock, as Jezabel hurried in ten minutes late. It had indeed been a crazy morning. She had forgotten to set the alarm, and all night long she had dreams of Michael calling her, Michael at the door, Michael starting to move his things into her apartment. In some of the dreams, they were fighting and in others, making love, usually with her realizing she was in pain but not saying anything about it. When she finally did awake for real, she looked at her clock, horrified to see she was due at work in twenty minutes.

She readied herself in literally less than five minutes, washing her face, brushing her teeth, throwing on an outfit and running to the bus stop. She brushed her hair on the bus and wiped toothpaste off her mouth as she crossed the street. This was the worst way to start a day, she thought, especially a day supervised by Sharon, a day when the lobby was crammed full of clients waiting to sell their souls for a quick financial fix.

"Take your time," the man said. "Really. I'm not in a hurry, and you will have plenty of others after me who might not be so patient, so please. Don't rush on my account."

She looked at him, studying his clean-shaven face to see if he was serious. He wore a small, kind smile, his graying blond hair swept to the side, his thick neck resting comfortably within the collar of the wrinkled shirt. She smiled a bit and logged into her system.

"Well, it will take a few minutes to get in here," she said. "May I see your paperwork?"

He handed it to her. "Here it is, such as it is," he said. "The address I have listed is only temporary, but I have a P.O. box as well in case you need to send me anything in the mail."

"Okay," she said, examining the papers. "So I should mark the P.O. box as your mailing address, is that correct?"

"Yes," the man said. "Word of advice. If you think your housing situation might be unstable, always get a P.O. box. Then at least you have a mailing address to list on job applications."

"I've heard that," she said, looking at him, understanding. "Thank you."

She didn't know why she was thanking him, but it seemed appropriate somehow, like he was trying to give her advice—or a warning. But right now, she appreciated any advice, no matter who it might come from. It made her feel like someone cared, but it also made her nervous. Did he think she would be in his place soon, having to use a P.O. box in lieu of a permanent address?

"Don't worry. I'm not shy about it. I've lived in some pretty bad spaces, and the hardest thing to do is to get yourself out of those spaces if you don't at least have the know-how to pretend you are not in such a space. Do you understand what I mean by that?"

"I think I do," she said.

The man leaned against her desk, on his elbows, his chin in his hands. "It's the most remarkable thing I have learned about this world," he said. "The world creates these spaces and helps you get there, but once you are there, the world would like to pretend those places don't exist. And if you remind the world those places do exist, you have then damned yourself to those places forever.

"So it seems best that if you do wind up in one of those places, and you know the kind I mean, I think, young lady, then you do best by yourself to play the denial game for awhile until you extricate yourself. Then and only then, should you choose to do something

about those places, can you really effect any kind of change. If you try
to do it while you are there, you are just damning yourself. Don't do
it to yourself, young lady. Please, if you ever find yourself in such a
position, get out first. Don't try to change the world when you aren't
in a position to do so."

The man's tawny eyes stared at her. His face looked sad and
intent and urgent. She nodded, quietly derailed, as if he were trying
to tell her something very important that could someday save her life.
Did he know her? Was she in some kind of trouble that she wasn't
aware of? Should she be scared?

Stupid, she told herself again. You're doing it again, getting
too involved. Stop listening to these people or you will go crazy.
After all, she hadn't done anything to put herself in danger, other
than arriving a few minutes too late. That, and of course, unplugging
the phone last night so she could get to sleep. She had meant to call
Michael this morning, but she just didn't have the time. She made a
mental note to call him before lunch if the crowd let up at all.

"Thank you," she said firmly. "I hope to not get into a situation
like that, but I understand how easily it can happen.

"Now, in reviewing your paperwork, I see you are working,
so you will have a way to pay this loan?" she asked.

The man nodded. "I tutor math," he said.

"Well good," she said. "So..."

He interrupted her. "It's pretty steady right now. Problem is
in summer. Some parents want their kids to keep up with tutoring so
they don't fall behind, but most, if the kids are that bad, send their
kids to summer school and don't want to pay for tutoring. What I
really need is to break into a new market, one of those newer schools,
you know the ones I'm talking about, the ones with real money. Then
I can get referrals and some students who are better off. And then..."

"Thank you, sir, I understand," she interrupted. "It sounds
like a fairly steady business, so you should be able to handle the loan,"
she said.

"Such as it is, yes."

"You've completed the rest of the fields, so if you just give me
a minute here..." She entered the information as quickly as she could.

Sometimes she felt like she spent her days in avoidance,
typing quickly, reciting disclaimers, dodging the conversations sure
to spring up in her office, trying to evade those connections that felt
inescapable no matter how politely she dismissed them.

I need to get out of this job, she said to herself. I need to get
out of this job.

There. She had said it, admitted it more bluntly than she had before.

I need to get out of this job, and I need to do it soon. If the clients don't drive me right over the edge, Sharon will. There is no way I can go on like this.

And then, to her own surprise, she thought, I am going to start looking for a new job.

A panic rushed through her fingertips as she typed. How? What? How would she explain her current position? What would she say about her company's reputation? Who could she use as references? There was no way...

No, she told herself firmly. There had to be a way. She would not be trapped in this office by an overbearing supervisor and a rotten financial image, not when she could earn at least the same amount somewhere else with a lot less stress. And while she was at it, she might as well face up to the fact that this job was starting to make her feel guilty. No, it wasn't just starting. It was making her feel guilty.

She had almost admitted it the day snake-boy came in to apply and never came back. She knew something had changed because she felt relieved he had not come back, she had mentally applauded him for not coming back. Her mind had muttered, "Good for you, snake-boy. You just got a new start for yourself. Don't let them ruin it for you."

Guilt. Why spend the day feeding it, lining Bobby and John's silken pockets with the lives of impoverished others, when she could be doing something else without that terrible burden? She had enough burdens in life. Why should her job have to add more?

"If you don't mind me saying," the man said, leaning forward again, pulling her out of her reverie, "you don't seem very happy with your job."

Jezabel barked a short, ironic laugh. And it suddenly occurred to her that the last time she had laughed at work — really laughed — it had been with a client, the little Asian man with the wife who was an accountant. She remembered that conversation and burst out laughing again. The man in her office cocked his head like a confused puppy, setting her off even more. Before she knew it, tears were streaming down her face, hot tears, tears she couldn't identify as tears of laughter or sadness, but it didn't matter. The man gave her an understanding smile.

"Knock, knock," said the all too familiar voice of Sharon. "Everything all right in here?"

Jezabel looked at her. Sharon was in gray today. Surprise, surprise.

She laughed even more now, holding her sides, gasping,

"Everything…is…just…just fine, Sharon." She wiped her face. Oh my God, she had better pull it together. She was losing it for sure. She giggled once more. "Just fine. I'm just printing now," she explained, trying to sound serious.

"And you are satisfied with the way your loan is being processed?" Sharon asked the man.

The man nodded sagely. "I am quite sure she is doing a fine job and I have to admit, the laughter has added a rather different dimension to my day, and I am not unhappy about it."

"I see," Sharon said, taken aback by eloquent speech that rivaled her own. "Well, I just wanted to be sure. We are quite concerned about the happiness of our clients."

"Well, then, kind lady," said the man in a tone Jezabel wasn't sure he meant as sarcastic or serious, "be comforted that I am quite satisfied."

Sharon nodded and returned to her own office.

Jezabel gave the man an appreciative look.

"I see you have adequate supervision."

"You might say that," Jezabel said and giggled again, trying to keep it quieter.

"Well that explains your current…disposition," he said. "I do hope you are able to find whatever it is you are looking for."

"Can I ask you…what made you think I was looking for something else?" she asked.

"My dear," he said, "I have worn that same expression you had on your face so many times in my life, I can barely count that high, and I am a math tutor.

"What human being has not resented the shackles he has been given to wear and then told to appear gracious while wearing them?"

She wondered if he were quoting a book or if he just enjoyed dramatically spouting off now and then. Either way, she appreciated his words and greatly appreciated the fact that someone else might recognize her position as one of imprisonment. "Thank you," she said again. "I am hoping to make some changes, but I haven't been sure how to go about it. I hope I can do something soon," she added. "Because…"

"…because your patience is running out?" he asked. "Because you have reached that point where you question if you can take another moment? Because you are wondering why you were put here on this Earth, if God had some kind of vendetta to settle in creating you, if this place is your version of Purgatory?"

She looked at him, blinked. "Well, maybe not all that, but some, yes," she said. She was getting that feeling again that she had allowed this man to step past a certain line, and now it was going to become more obvious why he would push that line to begin with and why he had ended up at her desk in the first place. She suddenly suspected he was not all he said he was, but that the other thing he was was not a bad thing.

His face remained kind and eager enough, however, and she was certain if he were a wacko, he was a harmless one. Still, she didn't think it would be wise to let him draw further conjecture on her life and decisions, so she had better establish solid boundaries once again and do so in permanent, black ink.

"I need to make some copies," she said. "Excuse me."

"Of course," he said, and leaned back again. She hurried away from her desk, and the man began to hum a tune Jezabel couldn't recognize but suspected might be classical.

The lobby sounded like a worldwide explosion of voices and languages toning down Tonya's English, letting in the little Spanish Jezabel knew, an occasional word in Portuguese or something Jezabel remembered Tonya had picked up just from working there. She patted Tonya on the shoulder and quickly made her copies. Charles was heading to the copier as well, staring open mouthed at the crowd in the lobby. The chairs were full, and a line stretched from the counter out the door, spilling onto the sidewalk. "What the hell?" he said to Jezabel. "Is there a sale someone forgot to tell us about?"

"Guess so," Jezabel answered. "I don't think I've ever seen it like this."

"Must be because the news of our fair boss has spread throughout the city," he said in the air of delivering a regal announcement.

"Charles, don't start. I was already late, and I am sure it has been duly noted."

"Don't worry, Jezzy girl," Charles said. "I'll stand with you in the unemployment line. Just me, you and a couple thousand other losers."

"Thanks, Charles, but I'm not ready for the loser line yet," she said. "I've got lots of planning to do, and standing around unemployed isn't part of that plan. And besides, who says those people are losers?"

He was about to come back with some wiseass crack, she was sure, but lo and behold, Sharon was coming out to the copier, either to break up the happy conversation or to check on her fans. Jezabel thought if Sharon spent less time patrolling and more time processing, the crowd would not be quite so large this morning. But it was none of Jezabel's business. She went back into her office where her tweed-wearing philosopher awaited.

"If you could sign here and here," she said, indicating the lines at the bottom. She prepared to recite the disclaimer: "And legally, I have to remind you that In-a-Pinch is not a bank. You are taking out a high interest loan to be repaid over a six-month period. You will be responsible for the principal of the loan, monthly interest accrued at 27% and the initiation fee of $75.00. If you miss one or more payments, we reserve the right to aggressively collect from you and/or the cosigners designated on your application form. Do you have any questions?"

The man stared at her blankly. "I'm sorry. I'm afraid I didn't understand all that."

She looked at him. Was he kidding? He was a math tutor, wasn't he?

"Sir?" she asked. "What part would you like me to explain?"

"Well, I suppose if you would repeat the whole thing slowly, I would appreciate it," he said.

"Okay," she said, wondering about this man. Then, slowly, she said again, "I have to remind you that In-a-Pinch is not a bank. You are taking out a high interest loan to be repaid over a six-month period. You will be responsible for the principal of the loan, monthly interest accrued at 27% and the initiation fee of $75.00. If you miss one or more payments, we reserve the right to aggressively collect from you and/or the cosigners designated on your application form. Do you have any questions?"

"Yes, as a matter of fact, I do," the man said. "But first, let me tell you how impressed I am that you can say that whole thing verbatim without missing one word." He paused. "Now, what exactly do 'they' do to collect on these loans?"

She was silent. "Well, um, I think they call and send you letters, and of course they can ruin your credit. I have never gotten into that part of the business, so I don't really know."

"With all due respect, miss, I am quite sure your clients could care less about their credit being ruined. What, then, motivates them to pay if they are bound and determined not to?"

She felt shaky all of a sudden, as if this was one of the things he had been warning her about. Ridiculous, she thought. This man was just intelligent, inquisitive and more than just a bit eccentric. He wanted to know details she was not privy to, and the best she could do for herself was to explain she was not included in the crowd of "need to know."

"I'm really sorry, sir, but I don't know."

"Well, who might?" he asked.

She paused.

Before, if anyone asked difficult questions (which was not often), she would refer people to the owners, give them a sticky note with Bobby and John's alternate office phone number on it. The clients usually were happy with this answer and signed anyway, even before actually getting their specific answers. Jezabel had the feeling this man would not be so easily pacified, however.

"Well there are the owners but…" she stopped, suddenly thinking. "But really, you probably would have to speak with my supervisor, Sharon Stuart."

The man nodded. "I would like that very much," he said.

"One moment, please, sir," she said.

She walked back to Sharon's office where Sharon was putting forth the usual questions, this time to a lady holding an infant. The infant cried now and then, and the lady, dressed in Middle Eastern garb, bounced the infant on her brightly robed legs and gently mumbled, "shhhhhh, little one, shhhhhhhhh."

"Excuse me, Sharon," Jezabel said, knocking on the open door. "Jezabel, I am with a client right now," she said in a brittle tone. "It will have to wait."

"I have a situation," said Jezabel, looking Sharon in the eye. Sharon put down her pen.

"What is it?" Sharon asked.

"My client would like to ask some very specific questions of the person who is in charge."

"Oh," said Sharon. The "person who is in charge" bit had obviously piqued her interest.

Sharon paused. "Well, in that case, if you will tell him I will be right with him, I would appreciate it."

"Okay," said Jezabel.

Jezabel walked back into her office. "She will be with you shortly," she told the man.

"Would you care for a cup of coffee?" she asked brightly, suddenly smiling. She loved the idea of putting Sharon on the spot, but there was something else making her happy, something touching the edges of her mind, but just softly enough to elude her.

"That sounds absolutely wonderful," he said. "Thank you. As I said before, I am not in a hurry, and I could use something warm."

"Then I will be right back," said Jezabel.

Jezabel suddenly felt like dancing out the door into the lobby.

She hummed "Greensleeves" as she poured the coffee into the little foam cup. She had forgotten to ask the man if he liked cream or sugar, so she poured some powdered cream into another cup, threw a couple of packets of various sweeteners on top and stuck a stirrer in.

She was about to carry both cups back to her office, a little smile still on her face, when Charles stood in front of her, blocking her route.

"Okay, you look way too amused, especially considering the way you rolled in here this morning. It's time you talked," he said leaning close to her to overcome the din of the line in the lobby without raising the gossip alert.

Jezabel smiled fake-sweetly at him. "What?" she asked. "What's there to talk about?"

"Don't play that game with me, Jezzy," he pretended to growl at her. "You never smile that much in this place even on a good day."

Was it that noticeable? It must be, she thought. In fact, Charles had hit a kind of nerve because Jezabel felt like she didn't really smile that much at all outside this place either.

"Nothing, it's nothing. Really," she said. After all, what was it anyway, other than her own satisfaction at being able to refer a problem to Sharon who was still basking in her newly-appointed glory?

"There is a man in your office who has been in there a long time. Now, either you two are making a date, or something more interesting is going on. And given the fact that you and Michael are planning to move in together at the end of the month, I highly doubt you're making a date, girl, so you betta talk!"

She chuckled, now, but felt herself wince a little at the reminder of Michael moving in. Why had she told Charles that? "Okay, but really," she said. "You're going to be disappointed."

"Try me," he responded, folding his arms and waiting.

Beyond Tonya's desk, a loud conversation had erupted among some Spanish speaking clients.

Two babies started to cry, the one in Sharon's office, the other in the lobby. A little black boy and an Indian girl raced each other from one end of the lobby to the other, a pale girl about ten cheering them on until Tonya yelled out, "Hey, you need to stop that! Stop that now!"

"The man in my office doesn't want to sign until he knows more about the collections process. I didn't know what else to say to him, so…"

Charles's face broke into a grin that threatened to take over the entire office. "You referred him to Sharon," he said.

"Yes," said Jezabel, perfectly serious.

He burst out laughing, slapping his knee. "Oh…oh Jezzy, I gotta thank you for that, girl! You just made my whole freaking morning! First of the real work heading her way, all right. Rev it on up! Send 'er more!"

He was still laughing open-mouthed as he made his way back to his office. Tonya looked over. Jezabel shrugged and walked back into her own office. She handed the man his two cups.

"Sir," she said, I forgot to ask you how you took your coffee, so I got you the fixings here."

"I thank you," he said. "Now, I know you have a room full of people out there, and that might not end up being a good thing, so how about I take a seat in the lobby and let you get to your next client while I wait for…what is her name?"

"Sharon," Jezabel said. "Sharon Stuart."

"Yes. I am sure you can let Ms. Stuart know I am waiting for her in the lobby," he said. He stirred his coffee, dumped the extra cup in the trash, nodded to Jezabel and walked out of her office.

Jezabel jotted down the man's location on a post-it note. She walked into Sharon's office, and without knocking, leaned past the woman and her crying baby and stuck the note in the center of Sharon's desk. Sharon shot Jezabel an ugly how-dare-you-barge-into-my-office look that Jezabel ignored.

She headed back into the lobby. "Tonya, you can send in the next client," she said. "My last client will be waiting here to see…Ms. Stuart."

Tonya raised her eyebrows and then nodded.

Within the next minute, one of the Hispanic women who had been part of the lobby discussion walked into Jezabel's office. She carried with her the paperwork and a huge satchel made of leather and suede patches. The bag was cinched closed with a leather tie, which the woman now loosened. From the bag, she removed a small black, device of some kind.

"Hello," said Jezabel. "Please have a seat."

"Hello," said the woman. She had a slight accent, medium-length, dark hair, thick eyebrows, and severe, almost-black, eyes. "I want to discuss paperwork with you, but I want to tape," she said.

"Excuse me?" asked Jezabel, just now realizing the device was a tape recorder.

"I need record to give to my husband. He want to know everything you say, and I forget, so I want to record."

"Oh," said Jezabel.

For the second time this morning, she was faced with an unusual request. Just last week, she would have begged for something different, something to break up the monotony of this job. Today, though, after the trials of the past week, she almost regretted wanting such diversions. A few moments of hum-drum today would have been welcomed, especially considering how tired she was.

"Um, I guess you can," said Jezabel.

Sheesh. Was the lady working for Bobby and John? Doubtful. But, Jezabel worried, what if she said something wrong and the woman got it on tape and told the shifty owners? Worse, what if the lady didn't work for Bobby and John but was trying to trip her up so she could bring Jezabel to court or something? But that was ridiculous. What would Jezabel say other than what she said every day? And why would the woman bring her, Jezabel, personally to court? She didn't own a thing, other than her broken down car. Why was she being so paranoid? She told herself to shut up.

Paranoid or not, Jezabel decided she better stick to the basics: review the paperwork, ask about how the loan would be paid, get the signature, recite the disclaimer and send this woman on her way as quickly as possible. That was the strategy.

"Okay, can I see your paperwork?" Jezabel asked.

"One moment, please," the woman said, clicking on the recorder and placing it on Jezabel's desk. "Would you mind repeating that?"

Jezabel gave the woman an irritated look, something she rarely did. But then, she had never had someone ask to record a loan interview, either. "I asked you if I could see your paperwork."

"Please say it closer to the microphone," said the woman.

Jezabel couldn't believe this. But she did as the woman wanted and leaned closer to the recorder.

"I asked you if I could see your paperwork," Jezabel said loudly. Oh my God, Jezabel thought. Am I going to have to talk like this the whole time?

"Here it is," the woman said, handing the paperwork over. Jezabel scanned it. It figured. Line three, previous address, was left blank, and the current address was less than five years old, which meant the woman actually had to fill in lines three and four as well.

"You need to fill in your address history here and here," Jezabel pointed out. "Fill in the addresses of your previous two residences."

The woman looked scornfully at the paper. "I skip these," she said.

"I know. I need you to fill these in."

"I skip these because I did not live in this country," she said, slowly, like Jezabel didn't understand English.

"I understand. It doesn't matter where you lived," Jezabel explained. "You have to fill in the lines.

"I lived in Mexico City," the woman said proudly.

"And that's fine," repeated Jezabel, trying to make her tone sound patient for the benefit of the tape recorder, "But I need you to fill in the lines, or they won't give you the loan."

The woman shrugged. She took the pen from Jezabel's hand and filled in the information.

Jezabel sighed internally. She couldn't blame the lady for wanting to protect herself or for not filling in the information. After all, it's not like Bobby and John could run international credit information. They could do extensive background checks if they wanted to, Jezabel supposed, but she was sure they wouldn't bother. She didn't get involved in that part of the business, either, and she preferred not to know how the two owners actually verified the application materials. It occurred to her they might not do any verification at all, considering they had their collections gurus to back them up.

The woman handed the paperwork back to Jezabel who made it clear she was entering the information into the computer. She typed, tapping the keys more loudly than she usually did, and then wondered why she was bothering. What would the woman do, have her husband listen to the sounds of data entry? This was absurd.

"How do you intend to pay this loan?" Jezabel asked in her I-am-being-recorded voice.

"My husband. He pays," the woman said.

"What does your husband do for work?" she asked.

"He works," the woman said and folded her arms across her chest. She wore a cranberry crochet sweater, and when she pulled on it, the holes opened up, exposing the lighter shades of her belly.

"I need to know what he does for work, how he plans to pay for the loan," Jezabel said, patiently.

The woman sat, stubbornly silent.

Jezabel sighed. "Look," she said, "I know this is not fun. I know you are not here because you want to be here. I know your husband plans to pay this loan, but I cannot give you a loan if you will not tell me what he does for work." She added, "I'm sorry. I have to ask you that."

Jezabel damned herself in her mind. Why was she apologizing for having to do her job? She didn't owe this woman anything, especially considering the hard time she was giving her. Why on earth…

"Carpenter," the woman said, releasing her arms a bit and letting the crochet fall back into its natural, closed-knit order. "He a carpenter. Very good one. He work hard. Business no so good now, though."

"Okay," nodded Jezabel. "Thank you." She almost told the woman she understood completely.

Jezabel entered in the rest of the information, sent the documents to the printer, and went out for her copies. "I will be right back," she said.

"This mean we get loan?" the woman asked.

Jezabel nodded. She got up and walked toward her door.

Suddenly, the woman smiled up at her. Jezabel stopped. "Thank you," the woman said, grabbing Jezabel's hand.

Jezabel nodded. "You're welcome." The woman would not let go of her hand, so she shook the lady's hand and said again, "You're welcome." She gave the woman a limp smile.

It dawned on Jezabel that this woman was afraid, probably of poverty and homelessness, the same things Jezabel worried about, the same things too many people worried about. She made her copies thinking to herself how sad it is that most people walk through life being so very, very afraid.

The woman signed on the lines. Jezabel said the disclaimer. The woman asked no more questions, snapped off the recorder, smiled again and left.

Jezabel put her head in her hands.

Chapter Ten

That's what she needed, she thought, passing the man sleeping on the bench. A newspaper. The help-wanted page. She needed to take that first step and see what was out there that she could do. Maybe she would have time to go buy one before she went home. She had to go to the grocery store and…

She remembered then that Michael had her car. Damn. She had forgotten to call him. Or had she just put it out of her mind? With all the craziness of the day, the man who wanted to see Sharon, the lady with the recorder and the stream of wild-eyed clients who followed, Jezabel hadn't even had time for a lunch break, never mind for a conciliatory phone call to her boyfriend.

She really needed to talk to him, had to make him understand that she knew he had problems, but she was having them too, and they were all coming at the same time.

Tonight. They needed to have the discussion tonight. And she needed her car. Otherwise, she wouldn't be able to get a newspaper and groceries.

The man on the bench groaned and rolled over, flipping to face the back of the bench. One sheet of his newspaper blanket took off in the breeze and landed at Jezabel's feet. With the way this day was working and with what she was expecting from the visit in the park, she wouldn't have been surprised if it was the obituaries lying at her feet. It wasn't. It was the classifieds.

Motorcycles.

Jezabel groaned. That's the last thing she wanted to see at her feet, in front of her face or anywhere else.

She remembered the little rhyme they used to say: Michael, Michael, motorcycle, turn the key and watch him pee. The idea of Michael on a motorcycle scared the hell out of her, not because of the rhyme but because of his drinking. It made her want to pee.

She had spoken to him about that bike thing before. He had driven drunk several times but had never been caught. He wasn't worried, he told her, and she shouldn't be either because he was a good driver. She told him she didn't care how much of a good driver he was. Drunk people were not good drivers. He got mad, then, so she just dropped it.

Driving a car while drunk was one thing, but a motorcycle was even worse. Half of her didn't mind giving up her car if it meant Michael wouldn't get the bike.

She stepped over the newspaper and walked the path, the day reverberating in her head like an amplifier at a rock concert. Her brain ached from it. Her legs moved quickly, on their own, streaking past the usual landmarks of trees and bush, anticipating the fence and woods. She knew the bunnymoose would be there. It was just too weird of day for it not to be there.

She stood at her fence, and she waited.

The silence eased the thumping in her head.

She picked up the last evidence of frozen snow and melted it on her temples, easing the pain that had formed the backdrop of her day.

She closed her eyes.

She heard a rustle.

When she opened her eyes, she saw a squirrel. Nothing more.

She closed her eyes again. A drop of snow skiddled down her back, making her shiver.

After a moment, she opened her eyes again.

Still nothing. "Come on," she murmured. "Where are you?"

She waited a few more moments, and then wondered how long she would wait. The uncanny feeling that she had imagined the creature and the previous conversation started to nag at her. But what, she thought. She had imagined this thing three times? That couldn't be. She might be losing her mind, but she wasn't that bad. Was she?

She closed her eyes again, telling herself not to worry.

"Scuse me, miss," a scuffed voice said close enough to her face to make her jump. How had she missed the sound of someone so near?

He wore sunglasses and a tattered army jacket. She looked at his tussled hair. She recognized him from somewhere. Yes, that was it. The man from the sub shop, the man she had seen outside the entrance that one time. It was him.

"Can you spare a dollar or two?"

She had started to worry he was following her, but now, looking more closely at the creases in his mouth, the lines on his face, she didn't think he would care enough to follow her. He looked like he hadn't shaved since the last time she saw him, and his beard was growing in awkwardly, thin in some places, completely missing in others, patchwork, like a quilt gone bad.

"I'm...I'm sorry," she said. "I really don't have any money."

She really was sorry, and she really didn't have any money. "I'm so sorry," she said again.

"That's okay. Thank you for your time, miss," he said. He continued on, past the woods.

He stopped, and he turned back to face her. "Don't stay out here too long, now, miss. Cold out here. Long winter we're having this year."

"Yes," she said. "I know. Thank you."

The man turned around and continued walking. Should she call out to him, ask him if he had ever seen a large animal in the woods? She wouldn't have to be specific. Just a simple question, that was all.

Jezabel, she broke in on herself. Jezabel, the man is homeless and probably drinks. No matter what answer he gave you, it wouldn't be one you could depend on.

Jezabel took one more look into the woods, scanning the underbrush and the distant, landmark rock, turned around and headed home.

She listened to the whir of the computer as it started up. Looking around the spare room, the room she hardly every used, she thought she might redecorate it. Correction. She should decorate it, period. It was always just "the spare room," so she had never bothered with more than a pair of sheers on the window.

The rest of her apartment had walls covered in used, old painting prints she had picked up at library and yard sales, and two shelves, one in the kitchen, the other in the living room, with dusty knick-knacks she had collected over the years, some from the same thrift shop, but certainly not all of them.

Her mother was fond of sending her holiday knick-knacks every Christmas, even though she knew Jezabel didn't dust often. Jezabel felt these were remnants of her relationship with her mother, a mother she never saw more than once a year, so she kept them all and didn't put them away, even after the holidays ended. The other decorations got stashed in the closet of the spare room, hibernating for the rest of the year. Not that Jezabel had a lot of Christmas decorations, but again, these were things she had accumulated over the years, some from her former life at the dorm...was it really eight years ago? The parties the college kids and everyone else in the dorm threw around the holidays were something—lots of decorations meant to be disposable that Jezabel asked to have and never did dispose of.

The decorations held up year after year with careful folding and storage, and Jezabel liked them. They reminded her of the fun she had in the dorm, the supervisors who made sure all the students had at least one gift under the community tree and the cards posted all around the hallways. It was one of the few times she really felt a part of the dorm and didn't feel like she needed to segregate herself. Because that is what she did, she knew. She didn't connect, and a good part of it was her fault.

Christmas wasn't like that anymore, but she kept those decorations, the same way she liked to keep those old art prints, and the same way she knew she wouldn't get rid of the knick-knacks. They were part of each other, these little items that had been with her for so long, and she felt if she gave them up, she would be giving up what little pieces seemed to hold the stages of her life together. They were glue for fragmented years that had led her here.

The picture of her and Michael holding hands assaulted her from her computer screen. She quickly pressed the space bar to get to her desktop and tried to connect to the Internet to check her home email, something she hardly ever did anymore because she just didn't use it, and her connection was lousy. She told herself to stop putting off calling Michael and just call him.

She sighed and picked up the phone next to her. She heard it ringing and then his voice saying, "Yeah?"

"Um, hi Michael," she said.

"Who's this?" he asked sarcastically.

"I know, I know it was crazy today. Michael, I really need to talk to you...there are some things..."

"Michael, it was just crazy today," he mimicked her, raising his voice an octave. "You have no idea how it is..."

"Michael, come on. I really need to talk to you about all this and I didn't get to it yesterday and then I was exhausted when you called last night..."

"And you unplugged your phone. Don't forget to mention that little detail," he said in his own voice.

"Yes, because I had to get some sleep and I never know if you are going to call back again or not," she said.

There. She said some of it. She didn't know why she was so nervous all the time, talking to him about these things. That was stupid. Just say it, she said. Come on, just say it.

"And I need my car back," she blurted.

"What?" he asked. "What do you mean you need your car back? You just said I could use it."

"I have to go to the grocery store, and I don't have any way to do that. And I'm not carrying groceries on the bus."

She sat silent, waiting for this to sink in.

"Okay. Why didn't you just say so? I'll be right over," he said.

"But," she said. She gulped.

She knew maybe she should say this all to his face, but the fact of the matter was, she was too scared. Just saying it on the phone, knowing he would come over later, was hard enough. Saying it to his face where he could become enraged right then and there just felt too risky.

"Michael, we can't do this. We can't move in together."

"Yeah, yeah, stop getting cold feet. I'll be over in a few minutes and we can talk about it."

"Michael," she said, "I mean it. We can't move in together. We can talk about it, but there is just no way."

"I said we will talk about it when I get there. Now let me get cleaned up and I will be right over."

"Okay," she said, trying not to sound meek and defeated. She had to hold strong on this, no matter what he said when he came over.

"Go outside in a few minutes and wait for me there so we can just leave and get the groceries and I don't have to turn the car off," he said. He was trying to sound patient. "Okay?"

"Okay," she said again and hung up.

She sighed and sank back in her chair. What was she doing? What had she been doing these past two weeks? Had she been crazy even to tell him that yes, she had decided to let him move in, or was she crazy now, nuts with all the stress at work and the money problems and the clients and her boss and...and seeing things.

It didn't matter, she thought. She wasn't comfortable with him moving in, and that was final. There was no way around it.

She got up, put her coat on and went out the front door, waiting for him by the entrance. Less than ten minutes later, he pulled up and unlocked the door for her.

"So," he said without further greeting, "what's with the cold feet all of a sudden?"

"Michael, it's not all of a sudden. I tried to tell you this a couple of days ago, but it just kept getting crazier and crazier and by the time I got home, there was no time to talk about it, and..."

"Yeah, yeah, okay, I get it," he said. "So what's the big deal? What's happening?"

She rattled off the series of events that had taken place at work, starting with the snake-boy and her decision to tell him more of the truth.

"Now wait a second," he interrupted, "What did you do that for? It's not your business to be this kid's mother."

"I know, I know," she said, "but I couldn't help it. I mean, here he was trying to start a new life for himself and what a way to do it...to get a loan from Bobby and John. Then what if he couldn't pay it? You know what would happen to him? It might be enough to make him do things."

"Things like what?"

"Things like...like things that would get him sent right back to where he was. Maybe sell some drugs to pay it all off, then he would go back to jail. I just didn't want that on my conscience," she said. "I mean, he seemed like a good kid that just made a few wrong turns and was trying to get his life back."

She desperately wanted Michael to understand, not only why she decided to tell snake-boy more than she should have, but why that was such an important decision. Michael should be able to connect the dots — he had been in a similar situation, eventually kicking the drugs and starting over. Why couldn't he understand Jezabel's natural reaction to snake-boy?

They pulled into the parking lot of the grocery store and got out of the car.

"And then, I didn't know it, but Bobby and John were outside my door."

"Oh, great," he said. "And let me guess. They heard you."

She nodded, miserably. Dammit, why did she feel like she had failed Michael somehow? This was about her job, not about him. "But they said I usually had such a good record that they didn't mind a little slip," she said, exaggerating their charity.

"Yeah, right. That's a 'don't fuck up again or you'll be outta here' if I ever heard one."

Jezabel ignored him. "So then, they make the announcement, the one we've all been dreading, that Sharon is now the office manager."

"Okay, so? So you get a boss you don't like. So what. I never like my bosses."

"Michael," she said, "it's not just that. It's the boss, it's the business, it's the clients, it's what those loans do to the clients. I can't deal with it anymore. Michael, I'm going to look for another job."

"What?" he said turning to her. "You're doing what? Don't be stupid!" he exploded.

Three people by the store entrance turned to stare at them.

"You can't do that, not now. You've been there too long. The pay's good and you have some benefits, which is more than I can say for me."

"But Michael," she said quietly, trying to avoid the pressing eyes of the interested customers, "that's the whole thing. You don't have a steady job, and I want to switch jobs. This isn't a good time to make that move we're talking about."

"You're nuts," he said, grabbing a cart and walking into the store with it. "If anything, it's the perfect time, it doesn't get any better. Look, I'll have work in a couple of weeks now, you'll settle in with your new boss, and between the two of us, we'll make it. It will be better than it is now, you'll see, once you see how much money we're saving by doing this. I decided to sell the truck for parts, and that'll give me a little money in the meantime, and we have your car, so we're good. You're just freaking out. Now stop it."

She walked silently beside him, stopping now and then for milk or eggs or cereal. She passed a newspaper stand and quickly dropped a paper into the cart, hoping he wouldn't ask why she wanted it when he had never seen her read a newspaper before. She wasn't going to change her mind and just "settle in" with Sharon. No way.

They made their way to the registers, less than twenty items in the cart, two of those items six packs of beer.

Jezabel's stomach growled. She remembered she had forgotten to eat dinner, she had been so worked up over telling Michael about her decision.

She wrote a check for the groceries that came to more than she expected. It was always better to write a check. It took longer for a check to clear which meant, on paper at least, she had more money in her account. Would things ever get any better?

Maybe Michael was right. Maybe she was just freaking out over nothing and the two of them, collectively, would do better than either of them singly. It made math sense, and she read numbers all day, so she should know. But it didn't make other sense to her. She didn't know what that "other" sense might be, but she knew it existed.

Michael helped carry the groceries inside and put them in her refrigerator. He turned to her, grabbed her by the hips, and pulled her towards him, kissing her solidly on the lips.

"Look," he said, gazing into her eyes, "look at me now. It's going to be okay. I know this is a big step," he said, his voice deep, soft, cajoling. "But really, it will be okay. I told you about that guy and the job and I called him today. He says I can start in two weeks, no hauling. He asked me if I had transportation, and I told him yes, and he says as long as I have that, it's no problem now. He got someone else with a truck and we can both do the job, okay? Okay?" he asked again, shaking her by the shoulders. "Now stop worrying."

She looked up into his eyes, those eyes that reeled her back in, those eyes that could look kind when they wanted to, and she felt that same melting feeling she always felt when she was with him and he was being tender with her.

She should have just done it all over the phone, she thought, just told him to give back the car and go away. It was too late now, and he knew it.

She disappeared into his embrace.

The alarm clock went off, and she hit the snooze button. Lately, she felt like it was harder and harder for her to fall asleep, harder and harder for her to wake up in the morning. Maybe a sick day. Maybe that is what she really needed. She had plenty of time accrued.

She rolled over and reached for Tarika. She got Michael instead.

That's right. She had told him he could stay last night, her last ounce of self restraint gone. She studied his face in the half light, the way sleep gentled his expression and kept it gentle, even with the beard. She touched his face lightly, so he didn't wake. She snuggled closer to him. He was warm.

Maybe he was right. This was a good decision, and she was just panicking. She gave herself a few more minutes of bathing in Michael's warmth before she made herself roll out of bed, shower and get dressed.

She dressed in a suit today, even though the owners wouldn't be in. Might as well get them used to seeing me in a suit, she thought, so when she did get an interview, it wouldn't be such a big deal.

She rolled the newspaper up and buried it in her purse. She hadn't even had time to read it last night, not with everything else going on. She was out the door in time to take the early bus, which would make up for yesterday's late morning. She hoped it wouldn't be another day like yesterday. Another huge crowd in the lobby just might put her over the edge.

She found a seat on the bus and opened the Help Wanted section. Financial. She skimmed the ads. Nothing. Everyone wanted someone with a degree, and she didn't have one. Even the bank preferred degreed tellers, and if that didn't disqualify her, the note that said, "strong references and background check required."

She didn't know if her references would be considered strong or not. She thought about using Charles and Tonya, but now that

Sharon was her supervisor, how would that work? And a background check? Jezabel herself had nothing to hide, but would a bank really appreciate the kind of business Jezabel worked for? Would In-a-Pinch hold up to close scrutiny? That had been her fear, always, and it still worried her. Stop it, she commanded herself. You have to stay positive. Keep looking.

Window washers. Sales. Food services. Nothing she was qualified to do, or nothing that would pay the same amount of money she earned at In-a-Pinch. It was ridiculous, really. Compared to what Bobby and John charged their clients, employee salaries were low. And compared to the finance industry? Jezabel would have been considered to be earning skid row wages. But still, she got paid better than minimum wage, better than most retail or food service workers or other workers in entry-level positions.

The problem was, she might be able to work for another private lending company, as Bobby and John referred to In-a-Pinch, but she didn't want to. Nor was it pleasant to think about the owners' reactions when they discovered she had gone to work for the competition. No, it was true. She felt condemned to life in prison, and now she had a new, head warden: Sharon Stuart.

Jezabel stuffed the paper back into her purse. The bus pulled up to the curb.

Jezabel crossed the street and went in. Sharon was already there, pouring herself a cup of coffee in the lobby. They had both beaten Tonya in today, but thank goodness, the place wasn't officially open yet, so there were no clients waiting.

"Well, good morning!" said Sharon, as if nicely surprised that Jezabel was early enough to enjoy coffee with her.

"Good morning," Jezabel responded.

"I see you're early this morning?" Sharon simpered.

"Nice, early start, yes," Jezabel replied, immediately heading for her office. "Yesterday was so busy, thought I would get organized and prepare for today."

"Good idea! I like that spirit, Jezabel!" Good, thought Jezabel. Keep liking it, you phony bitch and leave me alone so I can do my work.

Wow. She really did hate this woman, didn't she?

Oh well, she thought, hanging up her coat and turning on her computer. Nothing she didn't deserve for the rotten way she treated people.

Chapter Eleven

The girl looked at Jezabel, or rather, she looked through Jezabel. She had this dreamy expression on her face, an ethereal smile, and a melodic voice, high enough to sound sweet, but resonating so you knew she was sincere. "I'm getting this loan so Joseph and I can be together," she said.

"Okay," Jezabel replied, "but how do you plan on repaying it?"

"Well," said the girl, taking her time, "Joseph works at the bakery, and he said he can work some overtime. I work at the flower shop, and I can do some overtime. So between the two of us, we can easily pay off the loan."

She added, almost singing, "And that means we will have already paid for the reception hall and the photographer and the cake. You see, the cake is separate, and we really wanted a nice cake. My aunt knows how to decorate cakes, but Joseph's bakery has someone there who has decorated for very famous people, you know, like senators and people like that."

The girl continued, "So the man who decorates said he would do it privately for us and give us a better price than Joseph could get even with his discount. You see, it's not the ingredients that cost so much…we could go out and buy those ourselves, but it's the labor and that artistry. There is an art to decorating cakes. Did you know that?" she asked.

"Um, no I didn't," Jezabel said, starting to type, half listening to the girl carry on with her wedding plans.

The girl wore her blond hair long, longer than Jezabel's, and it looked like she hadn't cut it in years. The waves, bumps and split ends gave her the appearance of a tousled seraph, her white face glimmering with anticipation as she spoke about the future for her and her love, Joseph.

"I didn't know that either," she said. "But I understand it now, after looking at all the beautiful cakes this man had decorated. You can see why he decorates for senators. He makes all kinds of flowers, not just roses, but lilies and wildflowers and orchids and all kinds of things that he surrounds the cake with. It's the most beautiful thing I've ever seen," she sighed. "And I just wanted us to have a beautiful cake like that. You only get married once, and we just want it to be the perfect day."

"I can understand that," thought Jezabel. But she really couldn't understand it. Taking a loan like this for a cake? It didn't make sense to her, but she didn't say anything to the girl who really believed "you only get married once."

She remembered the time when she was so sure she and Michael were going to get married. They had been about a year into their relationship. It wasn't long after the picture of them in Felonias Park. Michael called her and said, "Honey, I need to see you. I mean I need to see you now!" He sounded frantic with some kind of exploding joy. She wondered now how long it had been since he called her "honey" but dismissed the thought.

She had met him, though, in a quaint café about two blocks from her office. She waited in the dark little place supposed to be decorated like a colonial tavern. Stained, thick, wood seats, tables with husky legs, pewter tableware and silver candle holders. It was a cute place with brass dishes hanging on the walls, the dishes with scenes of colonial sailors and soldiers and farmers. It was the kind of place Jezabel wouldn't mind accepting a proposal in.

Jezabel nursed a cup of coffee. At that time, there was no Sharon to worry about, no model of financial perfection hovering about the lobby waiting to pounce on an employee who happened to take five extra minutes for lunch.

Michael slid into the seat in front of her. "Just coffee," he told the waitress.

"Hi!" Jezabel said. "So what's up?"

He grinned at her and was silent for a brief moment. He wanted to make her sit in suspense, but it was obvious he couldn't wait to tell her, and his mouth looked like it was about to burst open around the edges.

This was before the beard. Jezabel could read his face and his excitement, and she leaned forward in anticipation. "What is it? What is it?" she asked, dying to know.

"What if I told you I won the lottery?" he asked.

Her mouth hung open. "Michael, you're kidding me," she said.

He shook his head. "Nope. I'm not."

She wanted to jump up and scream, but she contained herself. "Oh my God! Oh my God! Oh my God!" was all she kept saying, holding her hand over her mouth. "Michael!"

He laughed. "Yup. I know."

"I mean…mean…how? I mean, how much?"

"Five thousand," he said.

"Oh my God! Michael!" she half screamed.

Sad, she thought now, how excited she had been. Five thousand dollars. It had sounded like so much money at the time, enough to get married on, enough to live on for a long while. That coffee seemed to last forever, the planning even longer. By the time they left the café, Jezabel could picture their future together. She had been what then, twenty-two or so? It seemed like forever ago.

"And we have the most beautiful church in the city," the marrying girl said, breaking Jezabel's memory in two. "Do you know the shrine of Saint Mary? Well it practically is a Cathedral, isn't it? That's where we want our wedding. We've both been in there, have you been in there?"

"No, I haven't," said Jezabel, getting annoyed, but, she thought, hiding it well as she continued to type.

"There are these clouds painted on the ceiling, so as you look up, you feel like you are in heaven. And the angels are playing in and out of the clouds. Then there are pillars, and some of the angels are painted on the pillars as well. It is the most lovely thing," the girl breathed.

Jezabel wanted to ask the girl if the angels were going to help her pay the bills, but she kept her mouth shut.

Five thousand dollars. To this day, Jezabel still didn't understand where that money had gone. They had started talking about getting engaged. Michael talked about buying her a ring. He said he wanted to find them a place to live, the two of them, a nice place with new furniture they bought together at a store, not a thrift shop. For the next months, every time they got together or had a nice date, Jezabel had held her breath, waiting for Michael to show her the ring and officially ask her to marry him. And every time, he didn't.

New things showed up in Michael's apartment, a television, a stereo (the same one with the cords recently dismantled in his living room), a couple of new portable telephones. He got some work done on his truck and on the days he didn't work, he and Tony took some day trips Jezabel never knew where. She was glad he was having fun during his time off, and she didn't want to intrude. It was his money, wasn't it, so it was his business? It wasn't for her to tell him what he should do and not do.

"And then, at the altar are giant marble steps leading up to the tabernacle and behind the tabernacle is a gold cross, a real, gold cross. Sometimes around Easter they take out the gold chalices, too, real gold, not brass or anything else. It makes you feel like you are in Rome with the Pope himself."

This prattling girl never shut up, did she?

"What did you say you did for work?" asked Jezabel, interrupting.

"Well, I arrange flowers. Do you know the Smithston shop three blocks over? That's where I work. It is so perfect because I can get a discount on the flowers, too.

"Isn't that amazing? I want to arrange all my own flowers. I want Joseph to know I did it all for him, so every flower he looks at, he knows I did it out of love."

Jezabel wanted to puke.

"I need to print this out," she said abruptly, "and get copies. Be right back."

She hastily made her way to the printer.

"Well Jezzy, girl, what's up?" called Charles in his stage whisper, obviously not caring if Sharon heard or not. "What's the good news?"

Jezabel imitated her client quietly as Charles approached. "Well, I have this wonderful client this morning, and now I know how to put together a perfect wedding," she said in her own version of a high, la-la land voice. "Isn't that just wonderful? I just love how I get to meet so many interesting people here. And I learn so much. Do you know if you work for Smithston Flowers you can get a discount on flowers? It's amazing, isn't it?"

"Whoa, someone is in a very sarcastic mood today, I see," Charles said, amused. "This is so rare, Jezzy. I think I like it. Really. You must continue this way and go to lunch with me. Amuse me. Please. I need to be amused."

"Well," said Jezabel, making another copy and still imitating her client's high voice, "I will have to think about it. You know I wouldn't want to do anything that might offend my boyfriend."

As soon as she said it, she wanted to hit herself. What was she thinking? Kidding around was fine, but she was being obviously sarcastic even about Michael now. And she had sworn not to talk about her love life at work, especially with Charles. She had known him long enough for sure, but that didn't really mean anything.

"Hmmmm…Jezzy, I sense some underlying issues here," Charles said, imitating a television talk-show host. "Perhaps you can tell us what this is all about and see what our audience has to say?"

"No," she said, turning her own voice back on. "Sorry. Not for public commentary or amusement." She finished her copies and turned toward her office.

"Well, what about lunch?" he whined.

"That, I can do," she said.

What the heck. Her life was so weird right now, who cared? Why not make it a little weirder by adding a touch of Charles to it? Could be fun.

She entered her office and handed the papers to the girl, saying brusquely and quickly, like one of those disclaimers at the end of an auto sale commercial, "Okay, you need to sign here and here. And while you do that, I have to remind you that In-a-Pinch is not a bank. You are taking out a high interest loan to be repaid over a six-month period. You will be responsible for the principal of the loan, monthly interest accrued at 27% and the initiation fee of $75.00. If you miss one or more payments, we reserve the right to aggressively collect from you and/or the cosigners designated on your application form. Do you have any questions?"

"But I don't have a co-signer," the girl said, confused.

Jezabel suspected this angel from Heaven was often confused here on planet Earth.

"I know. But if you did, it would make that person responsible as well. Since it's only you on the loan, you are solely responsible."

"Okay, I understand," the girl said, softly.

Jezabel thought if she had to listen to that high pitched, sweetness one more second, she would have to slap the girl silly.

"Here is your copy, and here is ours," Jezabel said curtly. "You're all set. Have a nice day."

The girl looked at Jezabel and blinked her blue eyes at her. "Is that all I have to do?" she asked.

Jezabel nodded. "You're done."

"Oh, well, okay. Thank you." The girl picked up her coat and stumbled a step. "And you...you have a nice day, too," she said nervously. She folded up her copies and scrambled out of the office.

Thank God, Jezabel thought. She wished she could have been nicer to the girl, but really, one more minute of that and...

"Jezabel, I would like to speak with you a moment if you could, please."

The voice came from Sharon. How long had she been there? Or had she gone so far as to bug her office so she could listen in on her meetings with clients?

"Just wrapping up with a client," Jezabel said, "and I there are at least three waiting in the lobby."

"Well, they can wait a few minutes more," Sharon said, matter-of-factly. "I heard you working with that young woman."

"The one who just left?" Jezabel asked, even though she already knew the answer.

"Yes, the one who just left," Sharon repeated, patiently. "You were a little abrupt with her, not your usual style," she said.

Jezabel wanted to laugh. Not her usual style? What did Sharon know about her usual style? And didn't she, Jezabel, just get chastised for not being abrupt enough with snake-boy, who never did come back? What was this?

"As you know, we need to make our clients feel as comfortable as possible as we maintain our standards. I think that young woman could have used a little more courtesy, don't you think? A little congratulations?"

Congratulations? Was Sharon kidding? "Well, she signed," said Jezabel.

"Oh yes, I know she signed," Sharon said. "But we don't want to be known as the company that just wants people to sign on the dotted line, now, do we?"

Jezabel assumed it was a rhetorical question and didn't answer. "We want to be different from those other companies. We want people to know we care and that there is a reason to come here instead of going there. Wouldn't you agree?"

It was all Jezabel could do to restrain her laughter now, which was bubbling up in that crazy way laughter does when the world seems to have tipped upside down and everything looks like a bizarre parody of itself. Sharon wanted to make In-a-Pinch look like the "good guy." Oh my God. That really is funny. And the idea of Sharon changing the company image. Jezabel nodded, not trusting the laughter, sure it would erupt all over Sharon's lapel.

"So I think we need to have a plan for you," Sharon said, her low tone sounding monotonous and unfriendly but still professionally soft. "We will write something up so we know what your goals are," she said. "How does that sound?"

"Fine," said Jezabel who didn't really follow what Sharon was saying. She willed herself to care, but she couldn't.

"We will make some number quotas for you. I would like to see you closing thirty people a day."

"What?" Jezabel asked, paying attention now. "Thirty people a day?"

"That should be a reasonable amount, given all the clients we have. You said yourself there are three waiting right now."

"But thirty? There's no way I can do that. And there's no way you can know if all those people will be in on a particular day."

"Well, we will shoot for an average of thirty," Sharon

explained. "We will look at how your overall month is going, and then…"

"What's my average right now?" Jezabel interrupted.

"Twenty," Sharon said, looking Jezabel intently in the eye.

"So you want me to double that?"

Sharon blinked. "Yes," she said.

"But what about the image thing you just mentioned. You know, that thing about not wanting to make us seem like we just want people to sign."

"Increasing your productivity doesn't mean you have to stifle a friendly, caring demeanor. You should never do that."

Jezabel did laugh then. It came out as a gargled, gruff, ha! She shook her head.

This lady was nuts. If she had another job, Jezabel thought, she would walk out right now. Why deal with this? Charles and Tonya would give her good references, she was sure of it. The last thing she needed or wanted was dealing with Sharon and her unrealistic goals meant to do nothing more than tax Jezabel and impress the boss.

"Is there something the matter? Do you have any questions?" Sharon asked.

"No. I think it's unrealistic, though," Jezabel said. "Unrealistic, if not impossible."

"Oh, now you are just engaging in negative thinking," chided Sharon. "Of course it is possible. Look at how many people we had in here the other day. With a little more concentration, you could easily get those numbers up."

Yeah, thought Jezabel, and if I slept here, opened the doors early, didn't go to the bathroom and skipped lunch, well, maybe. But even then, it was a maybe.

"Let's set that as a goal and see how the first month works out, okay?" Sharon asked.

"Sure," Jezabel said. Whatever you say, Sharon, she said in her head.

"And Jezabel, I would like you to practice being courteous to the customers. Smile more and let them talk. Show them you are interested in their plans for the future. You are giving them something very special, Jezabel, a chance to fix their broken pasts and create a great future for them. Show them how happy it makes you to be doing that."

Jezabel couldn't believe what she was hearing. Did this lady actually believe what she was saying, or had she just not been privy to the collections techniques? No, there was no way with Sharon's snoopiness that she didn't know how collections were conducted or what the collections rate was. For the second time this morning, Jezabel wanted to throw up. And listen to the clients? Wasn't that contradictory? None of this made sense.

"If you'll excuse me, Sharon," she said getting up, "I need to work on getting my thirty clients processed for the day."

"Of course," Sharon said, getting up as well. "I appreciate your good attitude and your spirit. Keep up the good work."

Oh, I will, thought Jezabel. But it won't be here.

"I've just had it," she said.

She and Charles were eating BLT's and drinking orange soda across the street from the office. "I can't work for her, I don't feel good about what I'm doing, and I don't even know if I should be telling you this," she told him. She took a bite of her sandwich and raised her eyebrows at him, an admission that she felt she was spilling her guts to a largely unknown source.

"Okay, well," said Charles, clearing his throat. "I can see why you'd feel that way," he said, imitating a psychiatrist. "Let's process that for a moment, shall we? What led you to this point?"

Jezabel almost spit out her drink laughing. Good old Charles. He could be a royal pain, but when it came down to it, he just breezed through anything, taking it all in stride.

"Well, Doctor," she said, playing along, "I think the issue here is Sharon's strengthening grip on the company management and her apparent need to micromanage everything and every one in her sight. This puts us in a power struggle because…"

Charles interrupted, "You want the bitch to leave you the hell alone and let you do your job at least until you can find something better?"

"Why yes, Doctor, how nicely put," Jezebel said, grinning. Charles had hit it right on.

"Seriously, Jezzy, you know you are really smart. You got it going. You've been here longer than me, you have more experience, you can do better. I understand. Me, I'm not so sure yet. I don't have the time in that you do. But you, you can go anywhere."

"But that's the problem," she said. "I can't go anywhere. What am I going to go to? I'm basically working for loan sharks, I don't have a degree, I don't want to go work for the competitor, and I make too much to go back to flipping burgers. What am I going to do?"

"You need a career change," he said. "What about going to a head hunter?"

She hadn't thought of that. A head hunter might overlook

the kind of company Jezabel worked for, get her in with a legitimate company and out of this business.

"Good idea," she said. "Thanks. See? You've got some brains you're hiding in there, too."

"Why thank you, ma'am," he said, tipping an imaginary hat to her. "Now let's move on to you and Michael."

"Um, let's not," she said, looking down at her sandwich, suddenly losing her appetite.

"Something up with you two?"

What was she going to say? That she didn't want to move in with Michael, but when she was with him she changed her mind because he was so damn sexy? That she had told him he could, that he already gave his notice at his apartment, and now she didn't want to go through with it? That he got in very bad moods and kind of scared her? That he was unemployed and was driving her car, and that she had actually let him become dependent on her by letting him take her car, leaving herself without transportation?

There had been too much, too many emotions lately. She would have loved to feel close enough to Charles to tell him in words he could understand, "Hey, me and Michael...it just isn't happening. Work...it's bad. And let me tell you about this creature I saw in the park. It's really tripping me out." But she couldn't, especially that last part. She hadn't told a soul about her encounter. She was too scared the listener would want to have her admitted to the psych ward.

No. These were not the kinds of things she wanted to share with Charles.

"Got cold feet, huh?" he said, matter-of-factly. He bit the end of his sub and chewed, still talking. "Hey, I would too. Only natural," he said. "Don't be so hard on yourself."

"How did you know?" she asked, glad he had guessed only the less painful aspects of the situation.

He shrugged. "Common sense. You guys have been together for what, four or five years? Having your own space and doing your own thing except on weekends or whatever? Seems like a normal thing to me. I know I would have a hard time of it, living with a chick." He looked at her ironically, obviously trying to get a reaction from her.

It worked. "A chick?" she said, raising her eyebrows again.

He grinned. "You know. A dame. A wench."

"I'm going to have to hit you," she said threateningly.

"Okay, okay, you know what I meant," he said. "Seriously. That would be a hard adjustment to make. Have you guys talked about it?"

"About moving in?" she asked. "Of course."

"No, I mean about how you are feeling about it."

She looked guilty and shook her head. "Not really. I mean, I tried, but he said it wasn't really a problem, I was just nervous." She had to wonder about Charles sometimes. He seemed like such a joker, such a person not to take anything serious. And then again…

"Hmmm…" Charles said, putting on the "fake psychiatrist" look again, falling back into joke mode. "Very interesting. Some denial going on there. Let me think about it and I will get back to you. Because…our time is up."

Jezabel looked at her watch. Yikes! He was right. She crumbled up her wrapper, threw away the trash, and waited for Charles to put his coat on. They left the place together, crossing the street back to the present.

Chapter Twelve

Please. It had to be there. Even if it didn't really exist, she needed it to be there for her today.

Felonias Park was empty, and it felt colder than it had the other times she was here. The wind wasn't as strong, but the temperature had fallen again, and Jezabel had to be sure to cover her ears with her scarf, tying it in a tight knot behind her neck. She didn't like doing that because she wanted to listen for the sounds of movement through the frozen brush.

She remembered all the other times she had been here, walking through this park, with Michael, without Michael, looking for the mystical creature, and not. She remembered the homeless man on the park bench, the newspaper covering him, the one she knew for sure now was serving as blanket until the wind picked up a sheet and dropped it in front of her. The classifieds. Strange.

And the man with the glasses, the one from the sub shop with the army jacket and ragged pack. Was he really as old as he looked? Or had life simply led him to too many places, like the man in the tweed suit who wanted to ask Sharon questions, or the Chinese man counting, landing them all in Jezabel's mind which was currently located in Felonias Park, the one place where something imaginary still might survive?

But it wasn't imaginary. It's real, she thought. Whatever it is. It has to be.

She sighed a white cloud that vaporized almost immediately.

The park looked undisturbed, the bushes still sparse, the rock distant, the floor of the little wood frozen where the mystical creature lived. Yes, she was sure of it. She didn't imagine it. The creature had been there. It didn't matter if she hadn't seen it the last time or the other time. She had seen it twice, and that had to count for something.

She started to analyze why she wanted to see the thing so badly, but decided it didn't matter. Her life was reason enough to need it.

She heard the familiar rustle. She lost her breath in a brain-bursting excitement, so strong she didn't have time to examine the strangeness of it all, this ecstasy of meeting a bizarre creature who silently communicated with her. The why's and the how's didn't matter. What mattered was that it was here.

This time, the forehead appeared first, breaking through the sparse leaves with mottled hints of brown fur. Each ear cleared the branches, and the bunnymoose shook its huge head, casting off the inevitable itchiness of emerging through brush. The nose looked moist and shiny, and she noticed for the first time the sharpness of the whisker ends, like they would impale the leaves that got in the way of their tips.

The bunnymoose brought its legs forward, heaving its huge chest through, loping up toward the rickety fence, closer this time than the others, frightening Jezabel into further fascination. In its serene position, it stared at her once again, its ear hanging, reaching below the chin, its mouth, a thin strand of healthy pink, quiet and still, its big eyes looking at her soul.

"Can I pet you?" she asked aloud.

"You may," the bunnymoose replied, once again in her mind.

She raised her shaking hand to the bunnymoose's right ear and touched the middle of it tentatively. The fur was coarser here than she expected, even though she had touched the bridge of its nose that last time. The ear and face fur looked soft, like a rabbit's, but the rest of the body had the longer coat of a moose, and so she assumed that's where the rough texture came from.

Of course any animal that was made of more than one species would have a mixture of traits. It only made biological sense. Not that the idea itself made any sense or that any of this made sense. Nothing that was happening had anything to do with sense.

She plunged her fingers deeper into the fur, reaching the warm skin of the creature, and watched as it suddenly blinked, as if in surprised pleasure. She scratched it like she did Tarika when Tarika was in the mood for such a touch. The bunnyoose blinked again.

"Thank you," it said. "It has been a long time since someone has scratched my ears."

"How long?" Jezabel asked, softly.

"Decades."

She was silent, mulling this over, curious how old the creature was and how it had avoided detection this long.

"Yes," said the bunnymoose in her mind, "it has indeed been a long time, and I suspect it will be a long time again."

"Why do you say that?" asked Jezabel, now stroking the length of its ear.

"I must migrate," it said.

"Why?" she asked quickly.

She felt a kind of panic well up in her that she had not felt since her mother had announced her move.

"It is what I must do," said the bunnymoose, "if I want to live."

"Well, what is it?" Jezabel said, hearing a kind of whine in her voice. "Is it the weather? The food? The park? What?"

"It is merely my time is all," the bunnymoose said.

"That's silly," she said. "You don't need to do this. You obviously know how to survive. Please, don't do this. I know it sounds stupid, but I...I've come to look forward to you and I feel like I've just discovered you!"

"Don't worry," said the bunnymoose. "Silence your mind for a moment and don't worry."

"How can you say that?" she asked, her hand removed now. She had begun to pace, agitated. "How can you say that? Silence my mind? That's not fair."

"Shhhhh," said the bunnymoose in her mind again. "I say it because it is true. We cannot run from the truth, no matter how painful it might be. And my truth is that it is my time."

She said nothing. She stopped pacing and looked up at him. "So I won't ever see you again?" she asked, tears seeping in.

"Oh, you will see me again, I am quite sure," said the bunnymoose. "You will see me often, though I will not look like this. But, you will recognize me when you see me. Don't worry. You will recognize me."

She stared at him, tears now breaking through the damns of her resolve not to cry. "I don't want you to leave," she whispered.

"I know," it said back to her, but not aloud.

"I...I love you," she said.

"And I know that too," the bunnymoose said, nodding its huge head at her.

It lifted its hooves, twitched its tail and began to turn around.

"What will I do?" she asked.

"You will do what is right."

"But I don't know what is right!"

Back turned to Jezabel, it rustled through the woods, leaves clinging to its retreating form, the head disappearing first, then the shoulders, then the body, then the hooves and finally, the tail.

"Please don't leave!" she called out to it. "Please."

Jessica sobbed, her head in her hands. "Please," she said, shaking.

She eventually quieted, but had no idea how long it had taken her to calm to a quiet weeping. She did not bother to worry someone might have heard her talking to herself or sobbing in a city park. She felt alone, more alone than she had ever been in her life.

She wiped her nose on her sleeve.

She hugged her arms around her cold body, and she made her way out of the park, thinking all magic and hope had left the world.

She dialed the telephone.

She heard him pick up.

"Michael," she said. "We have to talk."

Her skin was tight with the salt her tears had boiled across her cheeks. It made her feel immune to his emotions, which is exactly what she needed to make this call. Her own sadness had evaporated hours ago, had turned to something like resolve and peace of mind.

"Bout what?"

"You and me."

"What about?"

"There isn't any you and me any more."

"What are you talking about?" he asked.

"You and me. We are done. Please don't call or come by. Ever again."

Before he could say another word, she hung up and unplugged the phone, grabbed the newspaper ads and sat down.

If he did come by, she knew she would call the police. But without a car and without the ambition to take a bus, Michael probably wouldn't bother.

Tarika jumped onto her lap. It was hard to tell which one of them was purring.

Epilogue

The article read, Former private lenders found guilty of loan, sharking, assault, blackmail.

Bobby and John Spellini, former owners of In-a-Pinch, a 'payday,' high interest lending firm, were convicted and sentenced sixty years following a three year investigation uncovering a series of illegal collections methods including threat, force, blackmail and multiple assaults.

Attorney for the Spellini brothers, Matt Ford, was unavailable for comment.

One other employee, Office Manager Sharon Stuart, is still being held without bond, pending trial.

Jezabel shook her head and put down the paper. She turned back to face her computer and began entering the information for the client in front of her. Outside, Tonya signed in more clients.

"Ma'am," Jezebel said, "I have to explain this to you…

"… Caring Places is a private, not-for-profit organization providing temporary shelter for the homeless. If, in thirty days, you still require shelter, we will ask that you complete this paperwork again and verify your financial status. In a moment, we can go to your room and get you set up. I am here to help you in whatever way I can, okay? Do you have any questions at this time?"

From across the hall, Charles' laughter poured like warm spring rain.

End

CPSIA information can be obtained at www.ICGtesting.com
Printed in the USA
LVOW112111171111

255412LV00001B/7/P

9 781608 300686